Other books by John D. Carter

Intelligence and Attention

Intimacy in Cocktail Lounges

Cape Lazo

Belle Islet Lady

CRAZY COUSINS

a Novel

BY

JOHN D. CARTER

CRAZY COUSINS Copyright © 2016 by John D. Carter
All rights reserved.

This book is a work of fiction. Any resemblance to actual persons, living or dead, events, or locales is entirely coincidental.

No part of this book may be reproduced in any manner whatsoever without prior written permission, except in the case of brief quotations embodied in critical articles or reviews.

Cover photography:
Robert Nyman ⓒ 2016, via Flickr.com
Used under Creative Commons License v4.0.

Cover and Book Design: Vladimir Verano, Third Place Press

PUBLISHED BY

John D. Carter

Belle.Islet@gmail.com

SECOND PRINTING

ISBN: 978-0-9940346-4-9

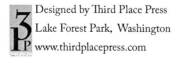

Designed by Third Place Press
Lake Forest Park, Washington
www.thirdplacepress.com

where the id was,

there ego shall be.

~Sigmund Freud

TABLE OF CONTENTS

THE ACCOUNTANT'S GIRLFRIEND	1
CRAZY COUSINS	21
LEFT BEHIND	51
POUCE COUPE CLYDESDALES	65
MEERA SANDHU	77
THE FIFTH WHEEL	93
METAPHORIC MOUNTAINS	95
MINERS BAY	117
CRAZY COUSINS OTHER SIDE	137
ACKNOWLEDGEMENTS	141
SECOND EDITION ACKNOWLEDGEMENTS	149

Crazy Cousins

The Accountant's Girlfriend

Gayle Thibault was the most beautiful woman I had ever seen in my life! We first met at my buddy Jimmy Swanson's twenty-fifth birthday party. Well, actually, saying that we met might be a bit of a stretch because there were so many people at the party, but we were both there. Gayle was sitting with Jimmy's sister Delia and Meera Sandhu. They were sipping some cocktails and discussing the gentrification of the old False Creek warehouse neighbourhood. I was all set to speak my opinion on the subject when Jimmy's cousin, Gerald Westonmeyer gave me a slap on the back saying, "Forget it man, stop drooling, you are way out of your league with that trio. C'mon, let's get a beer."

And with that I was swept away to the backyard bar and beer coolers where Jimmy's girlfriend, Breanne from Pouce Coupe—a suburb of Dawson Creek—was serving as bartender. Breanne was tall, thin, but buxom, and scantily clad for the party. "Mr. Morgan Elliott, pleasure to see you sir, what is your drinking pleasure?" Breanne asked with a smile.

"Whatcha got Bree?" I asked.

Answering for her, Gerald said, "Give the boy a beer, Bree."

"Sure thing, Molsons or Heiny?" she asked with a wink.

Answering for me, Gerald said, "Two Molsons please Mademoiselle."

We took the two brews and made our way over to a gaggle of geeks gathered by the barbeque. These were some of our friends and loved ones, congregated to celebrate Jimmy's birthday. Of course, Jimmy as usual held centre court and was pontificating about the problems with the current tax law reform propositions. Michael Lowie, one of our study buddies, was there with his girlfriend, Amy (real name: Amarjit, but you can call me Amy) Bains. He could hold his own with Jimmy while Craig Davidsen was impatient with Jimmy's rhetoric. Often it was impossibly hard to get a word in edgewise when Jimmy was on a roll and, of course, logical consistencies were not always mandatory, either. Jimmy, just take a breath, eh.

We were young accountants. Last spring we graduated from the University of British Columbia. Jimmy and Gerald landed jobs in the same firm on Burrard Street and I worked down the road on Alberni Avenue. It had been a long haul attending university and studying for all the accountant exams, but now we were working and finally earning some coins. When we were students we thought there were sporadic bursts of pressure, but working, now that is a different thing altogether, in terms of pressure.

"Geez Jimmy, they want us there all day, and every weekday, too."

Wardrobe issues were different, too. Gerald and Jimmy worked at an accounting financial firm where neckties were a really big deal. They both started buying expensive ties. Who ever thought neck adornment could be so expensive. Jimmy used to wear a beaded seashell necklace to school. Now he has gone all Holts and Rosens silk tie.

Spotting our arrival to the scrum, Jimmy shrieked, "Ah, yah, yah, if it isn't Monsieur Morgan and Chancellor Westonmeyer, defenders and offenders of the bourgeoisie and proletariat together, welcome, and welcome. Please help cross validate my assertion to our learned colleague, Mr. Lowie, who is struggling with the crucial concept of tax reforms at the provincial and federal levels."

"Yeah, well whatever Michael says, I'm with him," said Gerald Westonmeyer, that trailblazer of debate and deadly discussions.

Jimmy scoffed, "Thanks for the backup Gerry! However, may we inquire as to the parameters that comprise and compromise your endorsement of Mr. M.C. Lowie?"

"Yes, I know if you say one thing and Michael says the contrary, I'm going with Mikey based on probability theory and statistical accumulated empirical evidence."

"Ouch, and that is what?" Jimmy asked.

"More often that not, Michael is usually correct and you, my crazy cousin, are not. But, hey, Happy Birthday," Gerald said toasting with his bottle of beer in the air.

Jimmy has two older sisters, Colleen and Delia. Both are beautiful and both tend to dote on their baby brother Jimmy. Birth order is clearly evident in the Swanson family. Colleen, the peacemaking middle child, was always trying to reel Jimmy in. She had slid over to the edge of the scrum, "Jimmy, mum wants to do the cake soon, will you get everyone to move over to the tables?" Colleen asked.

"Marie Antoinette said, Let them eat cake!" Jimmy shouted, raising his arms in the air signifying an accurate three-point field goal. "Please, please proceed to the cake cutting guillotine."

We all gathered around the table to sing happy birthday and watch Jimmy blow out the candles. Call it coincidence or fantastically fortuitous but nonetheless I ended up standing beside Gayle Thibault for the cake cutting ceremony and speeches. And although Gerald Westonmeyer insisted I was out of my league with Gayle, I had to give it a shot by at least saying something witty or memorable to her. The best I could muster was a whistle and a shout saying, "Way to go Jimmy." I followed that bit of oration with a truly accidental bump into Gayle, nearly spilling her drink. "Oh sorry, crowd surge, I explained."

"No worries," Gayle said with an understanding smile and a lovely tilt of her head. Then Delia called her over to help with cut cake distribution. I was going to offer to assist her with cake distribution when Westonmeyer accosted me and enlisted my help in retrieving gifts from the trunk of his car.

Nothing is simple. What was supposed to "take a minute" ended up as a big production, and ain't that the way these things go. When we got to Gerald's car to grab the gifts, Jimmy's dad the dentist had been called out to do an emergency root canal. He was trying to jockey a couple of cars out of the way in order to extract his car. He was close, and we were trying to guide the little Mercedes Smart for Two out of the driveway onto the lawn, but it could not be done. As a result of realizing the futility of our efforts, I offered to give him a ride to the clinic on Arbutus Street. I had to do it, someone had a dental emergency, and I wanted good dental karma.

When I returned from the dental clinic the party was still reasonably rolling along. However, a number of guests had departed after the cake cutting and various speeches. Of course, just my luck, Gayle Thibault had carpooled with Meera Sandhu and Meera was scheduled to report to her shift working at the Vancouver Police Station on Cambie Street.

"You have got to be kidding me," I said to Jimmy. "You are saying Meera is a cop. She does not look like a cop."

"Yeah, what does a cop look like Morgan?" Jimmy asked.

"I don't know, but not like that sort of extreme gorgeousness, eh. And, besides, she was drinking." I replied.

"Relax man, she is a virgin and she was drinking virgin cocktails. The streets are still safe."

"Is Gayle a cop, too?" I asked.

"No way Morgan, she is a school teacher at Kitsilano Elementary School."

Wow, what a diverse group I thought to myself. I remembered Gerald saying those women were way out of my league and I agreed, but nevertheless, Gayle was extremely gorgeous. And I was not interested in all those women, just Gayle. I could not get the image out of my head of how beautiful she looked sitting there in Jimmy's backyard. I had to call her. Under the auspices of nothing ventured nothing gained I had to call. Of course, I had to first think of a call planning technique or some kind of introductory scenario. Jimmy's sister Delia liked me. She thought I was funny. I could get Delia to introduce me to Gayle. But, then again, we did not need an introduction; we had already met at the birthday party. Yes, that was it - that was my lead line. I would simply remind Gayle who I was and that we met at Jimmy's party.

I pulled out the telephone book and looked up the number for Kitsilano Elementary School. Nothing is simple. The first, second, and third times I called the secretary said, "Ms. Thibault is in a meeting, would I care to leave a message." I thought sure, just tell her an idiot is in pursuit, but rather I just said thanks, I will call later. Next I tried to secure her home landline number with little success. Who ever knew there were so many Thibaults in the phone book? I tried a process of elimination by locales and initials with no success. I gave up and tried the school number again at lunchtime. Bingo!

The school secretary said, "One moment please, I will page Ms. Thibault."

Nervously counting down silently in my mind: ten, nine, eight, seven, six, five, four, three, two, one, ten, nine eight, seven, six, five, four, three, two, one, ten, nine, eight, seven, six, five, four, three, two, one, ten, nine, eight, seven, six, five, "Hello, Ms. Thibault speaking."

"Oh, hi, hope it is okay calling you at work, it's Morgan Elliott, we met at Jimmy Swanson's party. Don't know if you remember me or not?"

"Yes, of course, I remember you. How are things Morgan, what's up?" she asked.

"Oh, nothing, nothing, just thought I would call, see how you are doing, you know, just saying hi, nothing of any consequence, nothing is up, just a social call."

"Well, thanks Morgan, nice to hear from you, but I can't really talk right now, I have some students waiting down the hall."

"Oh, yeah, yes, sorry, okay, don't let me keep you, catch you later." I said apologetically.

"No worries, call me at home. Do you have my number?" she asked.

I was not prepared. "No, I do not have your number, just a second, I'll get a pencil." I fumbled around searching for something to write with and then something to write upon. "Okay, shoot, I'm ready."

I wrote the number down twice. The first rendition was too wild and messy. I re-wrote it on a better piece of paper and with much neater penmanship. I carefully placed the good copy on the top of the "to-do" list on my desk. I had a tennis game scheduled with Craig Davidsen and I rushed to get to the courts—tardiness is too tacky.

I am not as competitive as Craig, but I was in the tennis zone and it was a good match up. Afterwards we went for a beer at Jerry's Cove Tavern at Alma Street. Craig was even competitive at beer drinking, but he is such a smart guy that overlooking his competitive nature was easy. His analytic skills were the best, almost as good as Michael Lowie. We discussed current events, work and women. Craig was an expert in all these areas and I needed the advice.

"Morgan, you are way too anxious man," Craig explained. "You have got to tone down the hype and you need to look a little more debonair and suave."

Of course Davidsen was correct. So maybe I was too apprehensive, so what? I thought about following his advice and waiting a couple of days before calling, but then why should I wait? Grandfather always said, "Do not put off to tomorrow things you can do today." Besides, Gayle invited me to call her at home. She gave me the number. Now she did not specify a time to call, however, a reasonable inference would be sooner rather than later. Of course good manners would suggest not calling during dinner hour or too late in the evening either. I chose eight o'clock as a good time to call. I got the answering machine, got flustered and hung up. Realizing that she probably had caller identification display and my name was now blinking on her handset I decided to call back and leave a rehearsed message. "Hi Gayle, it is Morgan Elliott calling, sorry to disturb you at school today. I am just calling to say hello, nothing serious, or no message of substance, just a social call. I will call again some other time, bye for now. Or, of course, call back when you get this."

Oh I wish I had said something witty, something with a little more zing, razzmatazz, or something a little more memorable, but the deal was done. The message was delivered, live with it. I thought about singing, but the goofy envelope may have already been pushed too far. I know not to ruminate, but it is just one of those personality quirks I guess. I sat there gazing at the telephone when it suddenly rang startling me upright. Call display showed it was Jimmy Swanson's cell number.

Answering on the second ring I said, "Hi Jimmy, what's up?"

"Hockey pool," he blurted with way too much volume, "where are your names?"

"Oh, sorry Jim, when is the deadline?" I asked.

"Now Morgan, the deadline was *yesterday*, and now it is *now*." Jimmy said with emphasis.

"I'll buy you lunch tomorrow and give you my names then," I said attempting to negotiate more time. It was the beginning of hockey season and Jimmy was the coordinator of the hockey pool. "I haven't put my team together yet and I need more time," I explained.

"Oh man, what have you been doing?" he asked. "I'll see you tomorrow, Fortes restaurant at noon."

"Sure thing, Jimmy, see you then."

We disengaged; I got out a pad of paper and began putting my hockey pool team together. Jimmy was a call backer. He never could let it go with just *one* call. Barely two minutes later he was calling back to remind me of the hockey pool rules and the absolute finality of tomorrow's deadline.

I started working again, but ten, nine, eight, seven, six, five, four, three, two one, ten, nine seven, six, five, four, three, two, one, ten, nine, eight, seven, six, five, four, three, two one, ten, nine seven, six, five, four, three, two, one, ten, nine, eight, seven, six, five, four, three, two one, ten, nine seven, six, five, four, three, two, one, ten, nine, eight, seven, six, five, four, three, two one, ten, nine seven, six, five, four, three, two, one. And the telephone rang again, "Jesus Jimmy, what now? I am working on the names!"

"Sorry Morgan, it isn't Jimmy," Gayle said somewhat apologetically, "I was returning your call, but it sounds like I've called at an inconvenient time?"

"No, no, it is fine," I explained my embarrassment; "Jimmy keeps calling and bugging me. I would much rather talk to you!"

"What names are you working on?" she asked.

I explained how the hockey pool worked, and Jimmy's self-appointed role of coordinator, treasurer, and general hockey taskmaster. It was only October and the preseason games were ending soon. The *real* season was about to begin.

"So are you a big-time hockey fan?" Gayle asked politely.

"Naw, not really, I'm from Vancouver, and we have never done very well hockey-wise."

"Never won a Stanley Cup?" she asked.

"No, Vancouver has won a six football Grey Cups, but never a Lord Frederick Stanley Cup. The Canucks joined the NHL in 1970, they went to the Stanley Cup in 1982 and were swept in four games by the New York Islanders, and then again in 1994 and lost a heart breaker game seven to the New York Rangers."

"Got a thing going with those New York teams, eh?"

"No, not really, we do not discriminate, Vancouver will lose to anyone. In 2011 the Canucks lost a Stanley Cup President's trophy season to the Boston Goons."

"Well for someone who claims not to be a big-time fan, you sure seem to know a lot."

"Got started early," I explained how my father had been a goalie for the UBC Thunderbirds, and he was a big-time fan with seasons tickets. "I was barely three years old when my dad had me on skates."

"Me too," Gayle replied, "I had hardly learned how to walk when they put skates on me and shoved me outside in the cold." As a child she grew up outside Thetford, and the Quebec Nordiques were the local fan favourites.

"I remember when the Winnipeg Jets moved to Phoenix in 1996, but when did the Nordiques go to Denver?" I asked.

Letting out a big gasp, "Oh man, *tabarnac*, that was a dark day in 1995 when they moved the Nordiques from Quebec City to America, for *money!*" Gayle exclaimed. "My Papa was just beside himself with anger. He even telephone Jacques Parizeau to rant and complain."

"Yeah, who is Jacques Parizeau?" I asked.

"You don't know who Jacques Parizeau was?" Gayle asked with disbelieve and some level of distain.

"No, sorry, I don't know, I'm from Vancouver. Who was he, what did he do? Was he the guy who moved the team to Denver? Or, was he the politician who would not support their staying?"

This opened a five-minute floodgate from Gayle's sovereignty side of the history of Québécois in Canada. Guess I touched a nerve not knowing Rene Levesque.

I tried to explain that with a combined population of just over eight million, in the fall of 2006, the provinces of Alberta and British Columbia actually overtook Quebec whose population was just under eight million. And this helped about as much as putting gasoline on a small fire about to intensify and explode.

"So, what does that mean? Quebec continues subservience to English Canada." Gayle asked with a rhetorical edge.

"No, no, I was just saying that under the auspices of representation by population we westerners have grown quite a bit since confederation."

"So what does that mean?" Gayle asked again. I realized switching the conversation to something easier and lighter like religion or the death penalty might be little more manageable than French politics and Quebec sovereignty.

"Hey, I did not know Meera Sandhu was a cop. She sure doesn't look like a cop."

"Oh, so what does that mean?" she asked yet again. "Morgan Elliott are you some sort of racist?"

"No, no, not at all," I pleaded. "Why would you say such a thing?" I said waving my hands palms up to surrender.

"Why would *I* say such a thing, you ask?"

"Yeah, yes, what gives the idea I am a racist. I am the antithesis of a racist." I claimed with as much muster as I could. "I am as open-minded as they come. A liberal democrat—not the political party Liberal, but the philosophical kind, I'm open-minded."

With a shake of her head, she said, "You do not sound so open-minded to me."

"Why do you say such a thing? I don't get it. What did I say or do to make you say such things?" I asked.

"Well first you slag Quebec, expounding on population by representation, and then you slag Punjabi people, saying they should not be cops."

"No, no, I did not say that," I said with a heavy sigh.

"Yes you did," she countered.

"Oh please let me put it in context," I pleaded.

"Yes, please, do put it in *context*," she invited.

"Okay, all I meant about Meera was that she seemed too beautiful to be a cop, that's all, no malice or anything."

"Oh, I see, no malice makes it okay, but beautiful Punjabi people should be what then? You think maybe a waitress, maybe a maid, or something more menial."

"No, no, not at all, I just think of cops as doughnut eaters and not at all like Meera, that's all."

"Oh, I see, Meera's okay, but it is cops you do not like."

"Yes, there you go, bingo!" I said, trying to move the conversation to another level or location. "You know this telephone-thing is not working too well for me. I am actually way, way better with face-to-face. Would you like to meet for coffee, brunch, lunch or dinner and continue at another venue?" I asked.

"Oh you know we French love multiple choices. Lets see, A, B, C, or D. I think I will pick *A*."

"Okay, choice *A* it is. Do you have any coffee cafe preferences? I like the Kitsilano Coffee Company; you know where Hilary Morris has the mural 'Meet Yew at 4th'?"

"Is that the place on 4th Avenue and Yew Street?"

"Yes, that is it."

"When and what time?" Gayle asked.

"Well, we could A, meet tomorrow morning before you go to school; B, meet after school; C, early tomorrow evening; or D, later tomorrow evening." I wanted to add choice E, all of the above, but I thought not to push the envelope too far.

"Do you not have to work or anything tomorrow? You seem to have a lot of flexibility."

"Yes, tomorrow is a flexible day for me. So any time that is good for you is good for me."

"Okay, your choice. What would be better 7:30 AM or 7:30 PM?" she asked.

Again, I thought about picking both, but was cautious about appearing too anxious, too over-eager. Quick strategic thinking suggested that the evening was more open ended so I said, "I pick the latter, choice B."

"Sounds good to me, see you then." Gayle said, disengaging the telephone.

Hanging up the telephone I felt pretty good. I had awkwardly secured a date with Gayle Thibault. WoW!

I do not know whether it is an exogenous or endogenous personality trait, but my people are always early for everything. Thus, I arrived at Kits Coffee Company fifteen minutes early, and Gayle was twenty minutes late. When we were UBC students we would wait ten minutes for a professor to show up to class before we took off. I gave Gayle one hundred percent more leeway than what we gave professors, and just when I thought things had gone south, she came streaming through the door.

Gayle Thibault's arrival was worth the wait. Of course, when she finally breezed through the door all I could think was WoW. Gayle was dressed casually, but she looked amazingly beautiful. She was wearing a white t-shirt, jean jacket, and faded jeans. Her long black hair was flowing, and she looked beautiful!

She spotted me sitting in the corner. I waved a hello and got up to greet her. "Hi, have you been here long?" she asked.

"No, just got here," I answered, "did you find parking okay?"

"Right out front, but, hey, when did they put in meters?"

"The parking meters are everywhere now," I replied, "The new mayor wants more money. Got to pay for the bike lanes, eh?"

Our first date went well, for the most part. We laughed about our telephone conversation's awkwardness and talked about problems with hockey, education, medical care costs, and urban planning. Things went well, the conversation was stimulating, and we were clicking along until we started talking about how the west side of Vancouver has streets named after trees. Streets such as Willow, Laurel, Maple, Ash, Arbutus, Balsam, Larch, Pine, Oak, Cedar, Cypress, and of course Yew, the name of the street where we were sitting. Gayle was saying how she loved the fall colours of deciduous trees in Quebec.

"I love the way the Yew trees' leaves look in the fall," she said.

"Yew trees are coniferous, not deciduous," I explained, "their leaves do not change colour, they are always green."

"Yes they do, you do not know what you are talking about. Yew trees are deciduous!"

She was adamant, but I knew she was wrong. I had spent so many summers chopping down trees, splitting, and stacking firewood with my Grandfather on the island. I knew about west coast trees. Although I knew nothing about fall foliage in Quebec, I knew with absolute certainty Yew trees do not change colour in the fall!

"Okay, okay, here is the deal Gayle," I began to explain, "I had a great statistics prof at UBC who used to say, "In God We Trust, and All Others Must Show Data." I will show you the data. There is no argument here; I will show you the data."

"Fine, sure, show me the data." She replied with a note of sarcasm. She was convinced that I was wrong.

The evening went too fast. There were a few bumps along the way, but it was good. We had an interesting conversation and I now needed to show her the facts that Yew trees are indeed coniferous.

Second date was a hockey game. Jimmy had landed a block of eight tickets for the Canucks and Dallas Stars game. I invited Gayle. "You know there is nothing like a quartet of accountants getting together for a wild time." I advertised.

"Yes, I can hardly wait," was her reply. "No, seriously, I am looking forward to the game, but I hate Dallas! Do you remember when they won the cup in 1999? The idea of hockey in June in Texas is just stupid," she said.

We gathered at Breanne's townhouse at English Bay for the pre-game pasta dinner. The plan was to carpool in Michael Lowie's mini van that he borrowed from his brother. Michael and Amy sat in the front of the mini van. Jimmy, Breanne, and Gayle were in row two, and I sat in the back row with Gerald and Nancy. I kept tapping Gayle on the shoulder until she turned around said that this was one of those things that I thought was funny but it was not funny, and nobody other than me thinks it funny *so stop it*. Of course, Jimmy and Westonmeyer said they thought juvenile behaviours were funny.

"Do it again," Jimmy whispered.

Gerry shook his head to say no don't do it.

I went with Gerry's suggestion. Okay, I know you are only young once, but you can be immature *forever*.

The game started poorly, and that is often, as they say: Par for the course. In the first period the Canucks went down three goals, but then they came back and tied in the second period. It was a back and forth penalty box filled third period with no goals going into the shootout. Five shootout rounds later the Canucks came out victorious. We had a jubilant ride home in the mini van. Although the next day was a workday, we went into Breanne's for post game nightcaps. It turned out as a great night and disengaging was difficult, but Gayle and I were the last to leave. Just before Gayle got into her car I gave her an article on the coniferous Pacific Yew tree.

"Thanks Morgan, it was a fun evening," Gayle said, giving me a firm hug before getting into her car. She rolled down the window, blew me a kiss, and said, "Let's do that again, see you soon," and she drove away.

I stood at the curb and waved watching the taillights fade. It had been fun and I did look forward to another rendezvous as soon as possible.

The all-important *third* date was dinner at my place. Some negotiations along with various venue permutations and we arranged a rendezvous at my place for a double date dinner and a DVD of Gayle's choice. Craig Davidsen and his new girlfriend Cheryl were going to join Gayle and me. However, at the last minute they had to cancel because Cheryl was called in to work the evening shift at the Museum of Anthropology. Gayle was sympathetic and suggested we hold off dinner until Cheryl got off work. Cheryl declined because it would be too late and she would be too tired. I convinced Gayle that we should go ahead as a duet because I had already purchased some perishable time dated dinner supplies. She agreed and all systems were on for the third date.

I had dinner all planned out like the invasion of Normandy. I prepared a Village Greek Salad for two, Granville Island Mushroom Leek Soup, my own special homemade three layers Lasagne, followed with homemade Apple Raspberry Cobbler with Vanilla Ice Cream. And although I had planned the dinner's timing down to a tee, I had not planned on Gayle's tardiness. Of course, from a statistical standpoint, I should have known she was going to be late. She was always late. She is a late person; if you want her to arrive for a seven pm dinner you need to tell her dinner is served at six.

It is not easy being anal. Everyone thinks it is easy to be anal, it is not all that easy, and you work at it all the time. At least I am not overly obsessive compulsive, I am just anal-retentive. Of course, I wish I was not so anal, but I wish Gayle was closer to being on time. I was cool and calm when she was fifteen minutes late. When she was thirty minutes late I became a little more ramped up and anxious. After an hour I had already started making telephone calls trying to track her down. I was a wreck. Finally, at eight twenty-five, Gayle came breezing through the door clutching a bottle of wine and an artsy DVD.

"Where the hell have you been?" I asked. "I have been worried sick about you. "You are an hour and a half late!" I exclaimed with a voice a little louder than likely necessary.

"*Sacre bleu*, no I am not ninety minutes late, you always exaggerate. What the fuck, relax, why are you so over wrought?" she asked. "You said come over for dinner. You did not say what time, you said come for dinner."

I know that English is her second language (ESL), but that is a language issue, not a time issue." I told you dinner is *served at seven!*"

"Oh so what," she replied, "why are you so uptight, is it an accountant thing, or just you? You need to learn to relax. Here, pour us some wine," she said passing me the wine bottle.

"No, you do it," I said, handing her a corkscrew, "I am going to rescue the dinner and try to put it back together."

I wondered whether it would always be such an awkward dance. Maybe it was me and not her. I did not know, but she bumped into me, we kissed, and nothing else mattered. She was just so exquisite to touch, even if she was chronically tardy, inconsiderate, and somewhat self centered. I had fallen in love with her. Of course, I could not tell her too soon. Cards to the vest, but I am no bluffer, in fact more of a blubberer. I had to guard against blurting out an inappropriate misstimed "I love you." However, I knew it was true and I could feel it from my core.

Things started to accelerate and we were going out regularly. Gayle was still chronically late, self centered and still inconsiderate, but I accommodated and learned to enjoy this relationship rollercoaster ride. She was the most beautiful woman I had ever known. I got tingles from her touch. I loved the way she carried herself. I loved her nose.

My apartment had better parking and was larger than hers. I had a bath and a half. Consequently Gayle began spending more and more time at my place. I gave her three drawers and closet space to make her mornings more comfortable.

I knew we had turned a relationship corner one day when we were walking down Robson Street and one of the teachers from Kitsilano Elementary stopped to say hello. Gayle seemed happy to see her, turned to me and said, "This is my boyfriend, Morgan. Morgan, this is Patti from my school." I shook her hand, said nice to meet you, and thought to my self, wow, Gayle just introduced *me* as her *boyfriend*.

Gayle plays squash proficiently. I thought it was interesting that she had such a strong passion for an *English* game originating from the nineteenth century. Nonetheless, I learned the game and began to play with her. I have played tennis since childhood, but had no experience with squash. It took a little while to get the hang of the racquet and the little court. I practiced and became quasi-competitive enough to hold my own with Gayle. We would play a couple of times a week. I liked the squash courts at UBC, but Gayle preferred the

Benthall Athletic Club squash courts. Parking is always such a hassle downtown. Gayle liked riding her bike downtown. It did not matter whether it was pouring rain or not, she would ride her bike.

Henri Lalonde was an avid squash player and a cyclist, too. Patti from Gayle's school was dating Henri. She suggested we all get together for a round robin squash match followed by dinner at her place. I said sure, it sounded like a good time to me. Little did I know that this was the beginning of the end.

Gayle thought Henri was a great guy. They really hit it off well together. Both speak French; both love squash and cycling. At first I did not think that much about their getting together to play squash. After all, Gayle had moved in with me. We were living together and she always came home at the end of the evening, home to me. I thought things were going quite well, all things considered.

Last Friday I came home and she was gone. Gayle had cleared out all her things and left a note on the table saying "sorry." I was surprised. I had not seen it coming and I was shocked, crushed, deflated, and demoralized.

Gerald explained in an accident your brain goes into shock as a defensive coping mechanism to prevent you from flapping around and incurring further injuries.

"What has that got to do with me and Gayle?" I asked.

"It means you are in a state of shock right now, but you need to stay calm and not go nuts over this thing."

"This thing," I blurted, "is my life! And, it is the death to the life that I wanted."

"Morgan, I understand, man, it is going take some time, but you will be okay."

Jimmy arrived already half-tanked. He had a backpack full of beer. "Jimmy, are you drinking and driving?" Gerald asked.

"No way man," he responded, "I am riding a bicycle."

We killed all the beer, ate pizza, and I finally got the guys to leave with my undertaking promise that I would remain calm and classy. They were worried I would contact Gayle and cause a scene, or do something stupid.

Of course, it was not even ten minutes after their departure that I was telephoning Gayle's cell phone trying to talk. Evidently there once was a way to get around caller display identification, but I do not how to execute such a call. She would not answer her phone.

I tortured myself with visions of Gayle having sex with Henri. I could not sit around. I had to talk to Gayle. I was able to get Patti's telephone number by back checking incoming calls from our previous squash soiree. Bingo!

My first call to Patti was a lie. I asked how things were going and if she was still seeing Henri. She said Henri had dumped her. I offered my sympathies and asked if she could give me his address because I had some squash stuff to return to him.

Henri lives in Mount Pleasant near city hall on Ontario Street. How ironic that someone from Quebec would rent a place on Ontario Street. Patti had explained that he only had a cell phone and no landline. I was going to go over and confront them. I started thinking over my tactics, but first I had to call Patti back and explain the truth. Historically, I was not a liar and was not going to start now.

"Yes, Morgan, I knew Henri had dumped me for Gayle." was Patti's reply. "I saw them in the school's parking lot. I am sorry, but I do not know you all that well and I did not know what to tell you. So I said nothing. Are you going to be okay?"

"Oh sure," I scoffed, "I am cool, this is no big thing. There are lots of fish in the sea."

"Hey, that is great Morgan, good attitude. I was really choked up at first, but now I am starting to get on the other side." Patti explained. "It really hurt at first."

"I can imagine, duplicity is deadly, betrayal is bad."

"Thanks."

"Sorry, I have always been an asshole." I explained.

"Yeah, I know, that is what Gayle told us in the school staffroom."

"No way."

"Yes way."

"Seriously, she said I was an asshole in the school staff room?" I asked.

"She said you were self diagnosed as anal-retentive."

"True, yes, that may be true only to a certain extent in some situations."

"Listen Morgan, you are a good guy, Gayle and Henri they are low class. I have got to go now, but call me again. We can go out sometime for coffee, a movie, or something."

"Yeah, sure, I will give you a call." I replied with little or no intentions other than to be polite.

I hung up the telephone and started crying. At first it was soft and it built to a crescendo with convulsions. I was hurt and I was not getting over it. I stomped around, but did not throw things around other than pillows. Wrecking my place would be stupid.

Three days later I called Patti. "Would you like to get together for a coffee?"

"Okay."

"Do you know the coffee shop on Yew Street and Fourth Avenue?" I asked.

"Is it the place with the mural on the back wall?" Patti inquired.

"Yes, that is the place, unless you would rather go to another."

"No, Morgan, Yew Street is great, see you tomorrow."

Crazy Cousins

My grampa told me, "Listen here, Gerald, families are funny, in terms of composition, constellation, and culture. Everybody has a family. Correspondingly, everyone has a family tree."

Our family tree is a little gnarly, twisted and maybe mis-shapen, too. Mind you, I guess everyone, or should I say many people, also report similar circumstances. Grampa often said, "Gerald, on our family tree, all branches lead to the tree's trunk." Gramps pontificated all the time. Most of the time I had no clue what he was talking about, but he was my Grampa, and I loved him. Gramps gets a wide margin, and lots of latitude.

I thought to myself, of course, all branches of the family tree lead to the trunk, so what. Who cares?

Our family tree's roots were hard to see, but above ground, that was a different story. Now, I am no arborist, botanist, or landscape artist, but from a visual perspective, our family tree has branches going every which way with what seems like multiple trunks, broken limbs, and who knows whether to prune or chainsaw the decaying parts, or not. Maybe diversity is healthy?

Jimmy Swanson was labelled as one of the "*crazy cousins.*" Dad demarcated that part of the family as "wild and crazy" but what did

I know? Jimmy and I were kids together. We played in the backyard while our mums made raspberry jam and canned peaches. Together Jimmy and I were adolescents; then we were college students, graduates, and the next thing you know there we were young urban professionals running on the career treadmill and climbing career ladders.

Dad was wrong. Historically, Jimmy travels on a pretty even keel. He was always a straightforward kid. Certainly some of the cousins were indeed wild and crazy, but not Jimmy. I can only recall two critical incidents where he over-reacted and went a little "crazy."

The first time was the morning Jimmy woke and found a city work crew installing parking meters in front of their family home on Third Avenue in between Yew and Arbutus Streets. It really was not all that unexpected; everyone knew the creeping parking meter syndrome was spreading all over the City of Vancouver. The mayor wants more money. Parking is a tax and more meters means more money. We all just dealt with it, got over it, and felt like it was just part of modern urban living. The bastards just kept getting you one way or another. And whatever you do, don't get him started on tax reforms and fairness.

Jimmy was calm at first. He asked the work crew what the hell they thought they were doing. And, in turn, they told him. It was at that point Jimmy had a bad reaction. It is not completely clear exactly what happened next, but when the police arrived, tempers flared and all hell broke loose.

It wasn't even noon when I got the call. Both, Jimmy and one of the city work crew employees were arrested for "disturbing the peace" or some other trumped up shopping list of charges the cops made in an attempt to calm things down. Jimmy claimed the worker was trespassing on their private property and the worker claimed Jimmy was uttering threats.

Both sides had witnesses. Both sides said the other started the whole thing by going too far with tempers and loud voices. The cops took Jimmy and the worker to the local lockup on Main Street to "sort things out."

Probably things could have been sorted better. Of course, too bad some sorting was needed in the first place. Cops, circumstances, conflict resolution, and Jimmy's current girlfriend, Breanne, from Pouce Coupe—a suburb of Dawson Creek—did not help much in slowing down this loaded freight train from running off the rails.

Cooler heads could have seen that if only Jimmy had calmed down quicker he would not have been put in a corner and required to donnybrook his way out of a stupid situation. When it gets hot in the kitchen, you should get out. But, oh no, not Jimmy, he was too manic and bordering on bad behaviour.

Guess the die was cast. The toothpaste had been squeezed out of the tube and we could not get it back inside. The eggshell was cracked and the yolk oozed out. It unfolded way too fast, and the next you knew, Jimmy was formally charged with a laundry list of offences.

Now on the Canadian continent, Vancouver is the farthest you can get from England, but the queen still rules and the prosecutors work for the "crown." And someone from the crown's office sided with the cops. Thus, making the decision to proceed with a formal charge of assault a reality.

Of course the whole thing was basically bogus, but what can you do, eh? We had to get a Howe Street lawyer to represent Jimmy. But, hey, what was the alternative? We did not want Jimmy to have a criminal record for something as stupid as assaulting a parking meter installation worker.

It was an expensive ordeal—outlandish lawyer fees—and in the end Jimmy "promised" the judge that he would behave better. He was put on a "peace bond." This meant he had to behave better for one year or pay one thousand dollars to the crown. It was sort of like probation, but he did not get a criminal record. As an accountant, Jimmy could not afford a criminal record.

We had both worked so hard to become Chartered Accountants. I thought the exams were very difficult. Nothing ever seemed that difficult for Jimmy. Nevertheless, Jimmy and I studied together with a small study group. Sometimes I wasn't even anxious at all until we met with the group. Anxiety could get contagious. We were always prepping and peppering each other with possible and probable exam questions and accounting scenarios. On the big Uniform Final Exam, which takes *three* days, at four hours a day to write, our study buddy, Michael won the gold medal for the highest mark in British Columbia. We passed and that was good enough for us. We got jobs as associates in a large downtown firm and finally started making real coins. The money made a difference.

Although the legal issues were bogus, the last thing we wanted was for Jimmy to get a criminal record. Everybody knows young accountants are notoriously wild and crazy guys just like Jimmy and I. However, wild and crazy is one thing, a criminal record is quite another, a definite career problem.

Jimmy's brush with the law certainly classifies as a critical incident and we were celebratory when the whole thing was history, but we were still pissed off, nonetheless. The stupid parking meters live on. You can pay by cell phone nowadays.

The second notable critical incident involving Jimmy acting quasi crazy came shortly after his girlfriend, Breanne, from Pouce Coupe—a suburb of Dawson Creek, tried to coerce Jimmy into marriage. The ultimatum could have been crafted a little more smoothly. Jimmy liked her, but he did not want a home in the suburbs, and he did not want to settle down to start a family, yet. So Jimmy became "single", again. The relationship crumpled and collapsed, but it did not have to involve all the drama. The relationship detonation was too loud.

"Hey, Jimmy, at least you don't have to pay any legal fees," I said cajolingly, "there is no need for a separation agreement, no alimony, and division of property is pedestrian. You are in great shape, man!"

He heard me and that was different than listening, but it didn't matter much. Jimmy moved on. He wasn't crazy, but he became way more adventurous than when he was living with Breanne. He started getting back into top-notch physical condition. It seemed like lifting weights, running, swimming, and hiking all took up Jimmy's spare time. I went along for some activities, but not all endeavours. And to this day, I still wish I had passed on the hiking.

Hiking was the second critical incident. I saw it coming, but I didn't recognize it until it was too late. It was a lovely late fall day. The sun was shining; the birds were singing; the leaves were changing colour; and daylight savings time was still invoked.

Jimmy waited until nine in the morning before telephoning. It was one of my few rules he complied with, especially when he wanted my participation in an adventure.

At 9:01 the phone rang, "Hey Gerald, you awake, man?" Jimmy asked. "Let's do the Grouse Grind. It's a perfect day for it, not too hot and not too cold, just perfect."

"Geez Jimmy, I don't know. How soon you want to go? I haven't had my coffee yet, and I am marginally hung over from Derek Morson's dinner last night."

"No worries man, the fresh air will make you feel way better—live right now!" Jimmy's persuasion did not move me much.

Jimmy is a gadget guy. He was the first to get one of the big brick cell phones, then he had tiny cell phone, now he has one with Bluetooth that works "hands-free" with voice commands. So I should have known better when I heard him say, "I'm in my Jeep heading to your place right now, and I've got coffee and scones. I'll be there in a flash."

I knew better, really, I did know better, but Jimmy started cajoling me that this was going to be better than our last kayaking sojourn up the Burrard Inlet where we got caught in a changing tide's current and pulled way off course for an extra three hours of heavy paddling. I knew better that time, too. It was a mis-adventure, and in the end, it turned out okay because nobody got hurt. That was always a major parameter in Jimmy's family. No one should get hurt. Teasing or debates (arguing) were okay, unless someone started crying. As soon as someone in the family started crying that meant you had crossed the line, pushed too far, and must stop. Jimmy's mum made that rule and it was always enforced.

Last summer, Jimmy and I had done some backpack hiking around Whistler and Blackcomb Mountains, and it was basically okay. No one got hurt. I was in better overall shape than Jimmy, but he was a maniac when it came to the pace. He pushed too hard and too fast, but I could keep up with him, no problem. I preferred to go a little slower, and smell the sage. I wanted to have a good time, not a fast time. Our styles were way different.

Grouse Mountain is one of Vancouver's jewels. My parents used to have a house in the North Vancouver Edgemont Village neighbourhood at the foot of Grouse Mountain. It was a great place with a creek running through the back yard, but my dad worked in downtown Vancouver and he could not cope with the heavy traffic on the Lion's Gate Bridge. In those days there were no cell phones or cars with fax machines so dad sold the place and bought a Dunbar split-level. Consequently, commuting concerns were behind dad. He no longer had to deal with the bridge's congestion, traffic jams, and "dopey drivers." Road rage ranges in various forms—latent and blatant.

I hate moving. I love stability. Dad did not mind moving. He moved a lot. He was a mover. Of course, mum went with him. Dad was not necessarily a dictator, per se, but he wore the pants in the family, and everyone knew it. He made decisions that affected others, but he was the decision-maker. George Bush said the same thing.

Jimmy's family was the antithesis. It is not that Mrs. Swanson was subservient or submissive to the head of the household: Dr. S. However, she was a force to contend with when she got going, and everyone knew it, too.

Jimmy's older sisters, Delia and Colleen, were gorgeous. They were always the epitome of cool and contemporary. Of course, Jimmy and I were always too young to get involved with any of their parties and girlie get-togethers, but we always gave them a good go-for- it, and they knew it, too.

Pierre Trudeau, one of our smartest prime ministers, once said, "Some people live at the foot of great mountains, but they never climb them." So with Trudeau in the back of my mind I succumbed to Jimmy's suggestion. The next thing I knew we were flying down Denman Street through to Georgia Street, through the Stanley Park causeway, and onto the Lion's Gate Bridge. Hiking was happening.

Jimmy slurped and spilled his coffee while changing lanes and honking at Saskatchewan tourists. "Damn flatlanders, shouldn't drive so slow, eh?"

It may have been another of Jimmy's rhetorical questions or a statement of fact. I don't know, because I wasn't listening. I was still daydreaming about Trudeau. I was also thinking about how this four hundred and seventy-two meter bridge, completed in 1938, renovated in 1998, was the forty-third longest suspension bridge in the world. It connected Vancouver to the north shore, and, of course, the foot of Grouse Mountain.

"Geez Jimmy," I cautioned, "watch out for civilians! You almost hit those pedestrians!" I said, trying to scold him.

"Naw, relax, not even close" Jimmy said, swerving into the Grouse Mountain parking lot. "Let's get started!"

And hence began the debate between me, myself and I: how much gear should I take; should I bring the back pack; should I bring two small water bottles, or just one? Of course, Jimmy is the opposite. He is a ready, fire, aim, sort of person. Sequential steps mean nothing to Jim. He does not debate with an inner voice. NIKE: Just do it! And then he is gone.

"Hold up Jimmy," I pleaded, "are you not bringing anything?"

"Nope, I don't need any additional weight. I am going to beat Breanne's time of sixty-three minutes."

Evidently, Breanne had completed the 2.9-kilometer Grouse Grind trail in sixty-three minutes. "I thought you were over her?" I exclaimed with an exasperated tone.

"I am," he replied, "but she did the grind in sixty-three minutes and I am going to beat that time."

I groaned at the competitive thought, but let it go because there was no sense in the debate. Moot points notwithstanding. We both stood at the base of the trail. There was a big sign for the American tourists. It presented the Grouse Grind rules—few paid attention or adhered to them. The sign said it was 2800 feet, or 853 meters to the top. The 2.9 kilometres translated into 1.8 miles.

We started off together, but it soon became clear to me that Breanne's time was as stupid as she. "Jimmy, you go ahead," I offered, "I will see you at the top." I was in no hurry, he was.

This was as stupid as the Vancouver Sun Run, which was a 10-kilometer road race down Georgia Street and through Stanley Park to BC Place Stadium, but there were so many people, pushing and shoving that the time was irrelevant. I quit wearing a watch. I went for a good time, and not a fast time. Whether I was two minutes or ten minutes faster crossing the finish line did not matter to me, anymore. I was long over that competitive mindset. Not Jimmy, he always raced the clock. And the Grouse Grind would be no exception. "Gerald," he yelled as he spun his way up the trail, "you are too slow, man. I'll meet you at the top."

Fine by me Jimmy, did I not just say that I will meet you up top? Again, I am here for a good time, not a fast time. Never, have I ever said anything pejorative about hyper-people? Its not that I like the fever or anything, nor do I purport to understand their mentality or motivation, I just think Jimmy and the hyper-people are too concerned with coming in last. What's the deal with competitive people? This human race does not necessarily go to the swiftest, but those who keep on running. "Jimmy, pace yourself and do not hurt anyone." I yelled as his profile fled into the distance.

Now I could breathe and go at my own pace. I enjoyed the freedom. Who needs the stress? Along the way I met some nice people from Newfoundland. Nice accent and all, but still I did not really know what the hell they were talking about. I could not stay ahead of them, or fall behind, either. We were all puffing and huffing, but moving along. I do not know how Breanne completed the course in sixty-three minutes, but I was nowhere near that time when I finally reached the top, emerging to see Jimmy drinking diet soda, and waiting to clock me in at "Eighty-one minutes and twenty seven seconds."

"Go a head, yell it louder, some people in East Van didn't hear you! I said with distain.

"Sorry Gerry," Jimmy was apologetic. "You did a great job. Proud of you, man."

Afterwards, while we were eating lunch in the restaurant at the top, I read in the information brochure that the average time for my age group was ninety minutes. I already felt good, but I then felt better than average, and then I felt like it was all too stupid to get sucked into. Not Jimmy. Although an idiot about time, Jimmy is honest to a fault. It took him sixty-nine minutes and sixteen seconds to reach the top.

"Jimmy, sixty-nine is divine" I applauded. For a while, when we were still teens and learned the sexual context of the Canadian Kama Sutra sixty-nine position, it became a mantra. But, not today, sixty-nine was not as fast as sixty-three, and the silver medal was not gold.

Jimmy took off to the restroom while I was finishing the French fries. Upon returning he seemed ultra-hyper, but these things happen with him. It's just the way his personality proliferates.

"It is still early, what say we take one of those hiking trails and go do some exploring?" Jimmy said with a smile.

"Geez Jimmy, aren't you bagged?" I asked, "Where do you want to go now?"

He pointed to a not too distant peak, paid the bill, and we set out. But first, I stopped at the gift shop to buy another bottle of water and some cashews. I stuffed them in my backpack, and met up with Jimmy who was talking with some skater punks outside the shop. They gave him some sort of secret vernacular handshake, high-five salutations, I don't know because I travel with a different crowd. You know, the firm hand shakers and Masons.

"So Jimmy, you know those guys or something?" I asked.

"Yeah," nodding, "I met them in the washroom." And with a wink of the eye Jimmy partway pulled out a bag of weed from his pocket. Wacky tobaccy.

If I was only a little smarter, but too bad, I am not, I would have got on the tram to go down the mountain. Jimmy, my most cogent cousin, pleaded, "C'mon Gerry, live until you live." The old Punjabi saying we got from his neighbour, Mr. Sidhu, followed with a firm-embracing hug, and I found myself wandering up the trail listening to Jimmy humming Bob Dylan's *"Don't think twice."*

Live right now, carpe diem, or Mr. Sidhu's "live until you live," always gets me. I am a sucker for that stuff. Mr. Sidhu use to feed us homemade pakoras and explain his philosophy of life. "You boys live until you live," he would lament. Really, what he meant was life happens now and do not wait for it to catch you. Or something like that. He was old, and I never understood a lot of what he was talking about. We spoke Punglish together, and he did not understand much of what we were saying, either. But, hey, it was Kitsilano, and we were good neighbours. I liked Mr. Sidhu's stories about New Delhi, Kashmir, and cooking. Ram das.

Jimmy took a detour off the trail, and I *knew* it was a mistake. "Hey, where you going?" I asked.

He gave me a smirk, and a follow me wave. Stupidly, I followed him down narrow trail, through some bushes, over a fallen log, to the edge of the cliff where we sat down to have a drink.

Jimmy pulled out the pot, torched a fat joint, and began a big Bob Marley draw. "Oh yeah, that is what I am talking about" passing it my way.

Now I have never been much of a pot smoker, I drank beer in college, but I knew this was good pot. "How much this cost Jimmy?" I asked exhaling, and passing it back.

"Twenty-five bucks."

"Is that a good price?" I asked not knowing of this type of commerce.

"Don't know, it's just the price."

Right, I knew that. Jimmy was not a haggler; he paid the price and got on with it. Don't dicker pay the sticker.

We sat on the rocks for a while and although it was a beautiful day, the sun was still strong; I thought we should be moving on because we were nowhere close to the summit. Jimmy agreed, stretched, got up, and started to go in the opposite direction.

"Jimmy, wait, you are going the wrong way," I explained and pointed to the correct direction.

"No I am not." He replied emphatically.

And thus the discussion began. I knew we had wandered off the trail somewhat, but I wasn't sure exactly how much or how far we had diverted from the main trail. However, I thought Jimmy was definitely going the wrong way.

"Yes, you are," I pointed, "We came down the trail this way."

"No, we didn't. We came this way," and Jimmy gestured in the opposite direction.

This is a neurological thing. Some people have a compass in their head. You can blindfold them, spin them around, and they still know which way to go. I was not one of those people, but for sure Jimmy was not neurologically wired for directionality. He is severely left-handed.

I might have been right, but, I wasn't one hundred percent certain, maybe Jimmy was right. Who knows, everything looks the same: green. Trail-wise, it was hard to determine because it was not clearly marked and we did not know which way we were wandering. We did know we were now going in a circle. We were back at the rock where we started. Some of the cashews I had spilled were on the ground from our rest stop.

"Okay Jim, lets go your way."

"Oh, yes, and which way is that?"

"This way, I think. But, I don't really, really know."

Although I did feel some slight level of panic poking at my cerebral cortex, I knew it was still too soon to get scared. We were okay, it was still warm, the sun was still high, but descending. "All right, we have got to get systematic about this Jimmy, and figure this out."

"Sure, what do you have in mind? Where is the path back to the gondola? I thought it was behind us. It has to be behind us. It cannot be in front, that would be a drop-off, wouldn't it?" Jimmy was starting to get increasingly frazzled.

"Just settle down Jim. We are okay. We just need to figure it out. This is not a big deal; we just need to remember which direction did we come from?"

The look on his face was not suitable for playing poker. I began to realize that Jimmy was starting to lose it. And this was not a good thing. I had to get him to calm down and figure this thing out. Nothing will be gained from getting excited and flustered.

"Yeah, naw, I know, I know" Jimmy said flapping his arms and pointing in the direction we just came from, "we have got to go back this way."

"No way, we just came that way." I knew he was wrong.

"No we did not. We came the other direction. Didn't we?"

"Okay, listen, this is the deal Jim. We are on a mountain. Every way we look, every way we turn, we think the down side of the mountain is the wrong side of the mountain, right?"

"So what?" Jimmy was starting to panic. "I say we go this way!"

"No way Jim, that is definitely the wrong way. We already tried that route."

"No, we went the other way." Jimmy was confident, but wrong, and I knew it.

"Jim we just need to regroup and figure things out. There is no need to get excited. We are going to be okay, but we need to get systematic before the sun goes down and it gets dark. Then we would be really screwed. Which way is west?"

"I don't know which way is west, east, nothing!" Jimmy said stomping around the twigs. "We are fucked. I should have brought the stupid cell phone. And, the sun is going down."

I could suddenly see this unravelling before my eyes, but I couldn't stop it. Jimmy was freaking out and I just could not say anything to slow things down, diffuse the situation, or calm him down. I knew we were lost, but I did not think it fatal. This happens all the time. People are always getting lost on the North Shore Mountains. I have seen it a million times before on television's six o'clock news. Tony Parsons told us all about it.

Search and rescue crews bring some fools back down the mountain in a helicopter and the fools are usually repentant. Oh, but how I want to be one of those found fools. Fast forward and beam me down as a fool. I will be repentant.

"Let's go man, no more standing around; we have got to get out of here. It is going to get dark soon. And then we are fucked with a capitol F once it is dark."

"No way Jim, we need to just stay still, and let them find us. We have to stop tromping around in circles, zigzags, running around with our heads cut off. We are lost. It is okay, they will find us."

"How?"

"They just will."

"Wwwho is this *they* anyway? What makes you think they are going to find us? They aren't! This is our mess and we have to clean it up. We have to find our own way out of here. Let's get going." His eyes now had a flare and bugged out.

"No way Jimmy, we just need to stay still and let them find us."

"Quit saying that, you idiot! There is no they, and we have to get out of here on our own legs."

I knew he was wrong. I knew that if we kept on wandering around we would likely just get more lost than we already were. We would likely end up farther along the path to the wrong way. Besides, there was no path to follow; we had lost any sort of path a long time ago.

"Just sit down Jim. You have got to get a grip. We can't keep tromping mindlessly around the mountain."

"No way man, I am not going to sit down. I am walking down the mountain and I will tell them to come and get you."

And with that Jimmy started to walk away. I sat on the boulder, just frozen on the spot, watching him leave. Saying softly, "Good luck, Jim."

I kept up a sense of hope that he would come back and agree that staying put was the right thing to do. So, I just sat on my spot for who knows how long. And even though I knew Jimmy was definitely long, long, gone and certainly not coming back, I held out hope that he would suddenly come thumping through the trees with his stupid grin and a story about how this whole thing was a lark anyhow. I held the hope that he would come back with a compass and the direction home. I missed him. I was alone, not lonely, but I was also starting to get scared. Thoughts like maybe this thing was not going to have a happy ending started to intrude into my frontal lobes, backbone, and stomach.

I wish this; I wish that; and of course, all the "if only this" and "if only that's" plagued me now. And although I was sitting still, everything was spinning all around me. "Stop it," I screamed at the top of my lungs, "Jimmy you fucking bastard, get back here."

A robin landed on the Douglas fir tree that was growing out of the rocks, and I started to cry. Just a whimper, at first, and building up to a full-fledged wail with pseudo convulsions and shakes from head to toes, I had lost my composure. When I was finished, the robin had flown away and I was still alone without a plan.

"Recalcitrance, recalcitrance, fuck-a-duck, get up, and figure it out," I screamed, trying to talk myself back down to at least ground level, "figure this out!" I knew I needed to calm down and not waste mental as well as physical energy on things that were well beyond my control.

The Grouse Mountain parking lot empties pretty fast at the end of the day. Jimmy's Jeep, just like me, sat all alone waiting for his return. But, Jimmy did not return to me sitting somewhere on the mountain, or to his Jeep sitting in the parking lot.

In instances like these, the authorities follow protocols and procedures. And this was indeed good news for me. Too bad, at the time, I did not know these procedures and protocols would get invoked. If I did, maybe I would have felt less panic, fear, and anxiety. While I was freaking out, the North Shore Search and Rescue Team were assembling to begin a systematic search party.

It was getting dramatically darker. My decision to stay put in one place still sort of seemed better than Jimmy's decision to blast onwards without a plan. However, I was also hopeful that Jimmy had indeed found his way to the main trail and had already arrived at the bottom and was mustering a crew to come and get me.

Jimmy left with the matches he had used to light the pot. Shit-a-brick, I should have got him to share the matches with me before he stomped off. Hindsight is twenty-twenty. If I had matches I could start a fire for warmth and a signal for the rescue team. There has got to be a rescue team. I was counting on that and pinning all hope they get here soon.

It could happen. Jimmy must be at the bottom of the mountain now and a rescue party is on their way to retrieve me. Life works that way. Jimmy has always been a lucky guy. Of course, he made his own luck happen. He was confident, a take charge man, a mover and a shaker, and a risk taker. We both knew we were lost. I thought the best plan was to sit still and wait for help. I just felt that if we kept storming along without knowing where we were going we would only dig ourselves into a deeper hole, and we might get farther out in the wrong direction. Lost is lost, but I did not think we should get more lost than we already were. Deeper in debt—lost in debt and just lost period.

Guess, maybe I should have gone with Jim, but staying still seemed the best plan. Splitting up was probably a dumb thing to do. Maybe he'll come back and get me.

In my mind I envisioned Jimmy finding the path back to the gondola. I pictured him meeting some other hikers and I imagined that they traveled together to the bottom. Jimmy told them about the cousin he left behind on a rock in the woods. But, the authorities convinced Jimmy that there was not enough daylight left to retrieve the cousin left behind. Leave it to the professionals. They know how to do it.

It was really dark now. I was cold, tired, and hungry. I had gathered a bunch of cedar boughs to make a bed to lie on and keep me off the cold rocky earth. At first I tried to make a lean-to fort. Jimmy and I made lots of forts as kids, but not today, nothing was going right.

I tried to start a fire by using a rock smashing on another rock hoping to cause a spark and light the piece of paper and grass I had assembled. This seemed too dumb to continue. Wish I had paid more attention at Cub-Scout camp. I was sure I had earned a badge for camping, but how do you start a fire without matches?

Jimmy and I had a great time when we were Cub-Scouts. What an age; what a stage? Jimmy earned lots of badges. I was not as competitive.

One time when we were at a Derek Morson party, Jimmy was trying to put romantic moves on Lydia Burgess. I overheard him tell her, "Gerry and I were in the paramilitary as children."

"Really, the paramilitary? Lydia asked, looking over in my direction for clarification.

"Jimmy, what the frigs are you talking about?" I asked. "When were we in the paramilitary?"

"*Cub-Scouts!*" He replied. "We were Cub-Scouts. We wore uniforms, earned stripes, badges, and we saluted the leader with the Cub-Scout salute. Remember the motto:

Be Ready Always. We were in the paramilitary."

Jimmy insisted Cub-Scouts represented a paramilitary organization and there was no sense arguing the point. Besides, Lydia moved on and was now dancing with Elliott Margolis. Lydia sensed that Elliott was smoother and more sensible than Jim. She smiled at me with a head nod.

Although I could not remember the Cub-Scout motto, I am sure it was not "Be Ready Always." For the life of me I could not recall the motto. What was it?

Sleep started to overtake my limited level of consciousness, and I slid into the land of dreams. It was nice. I was not lost and alone lying like a human sandwich with cedar branches for a bed and cover to keep my body heat in and some semblance of warmth. I wasn't scared or cold either. In my dream I was climbing the North Face of Mount Everest with Sir Edmund Hillary and Al Gore.

Labrador Retrievers are beautiful dogs. I like the way their tail is shaped like a rudder for swimming. And although I have never liked the sound of barking dogs, when I heard the golden lab, Ksea's yelps it woke me with a startle.

Emerging from the cedar cocoon I found Ksea the Search and Rescue golden lab jumping around, barking, and making loud yelping sounds. It almost seemed as though he was happier to see me than him. In a couple of moments two men dressed in orange jumpsuits appeared. North Shore Search and Rescue decals were on the hardhat helmets and patches sewn on their breast and shoulders.

At the rescue scene they diagnosed me with hypothermia. I was not delirious, or completely incapacitated, but I was not all together, either. I was up on my feet and wobbly walking around. I felt wonky. I sort of remember slipping, and falling, but not too clearly.

Before I knew it I had been taken to the bottom of the mountain and transferred into some big motor home trailer type office place with maps and charts on the wall. Guess this was search headquarters. I was expecting to see Jimmy. In my mind I thought he had given the searchers my location and that was how they found me. Jimmy, however, was nowhere to be found.

A couple of senior official type authorities were asking me questions. I was processing and responding the best I could. I knew I was having trouble decoding, encoding, and expressing my thoughts. Disoriented and discombobulated, but I was now warm and safe.

I do not remember bonking my head on the rocks. The paramedic said I slipped and fell after I had been rescued. I was trying to walk out on my own legs. Guess I had convinced the rescue team that I was okay to walk, but I was wrong, and I ended up leaving in a helicopter suspended stretcher.

Delia, Jimmy's sister, my cousin, came through the door. She was accompanied by a petite, pretty blonde RCMP officer who looked a lot like Karen the cop on Brent Butt's (seriously, that is his name: Butt) *Corner Gas* television show.

Delia, as always, but especially today, looked beautiful, radiant, and she lit up the room. She offered a firm hug and said softly, "Gerald, how you doing?"

"Been better," was my reply.

Turns out Delia had been the person to call for help. Jimmy had been expected to attend a family function dinner yesterday evening. He had told Delia about his plans to do the Grouse Grind and promised to arrive by seven o'clock precisely. When Jimmy did not show on time Delia had the presence of mind to check with security to see if the Jeep was still in the parking lot. The Jeep was there and the protocols were put in place.

Everybody was asking me lots of questions. The search and rescue authorities showed me on a map where I was found. From that location they wanted to figure out which direction Jimmy was heading. They were confident that it would only be a matter of hours until they located Jimmy. "No problem, we will find him shortly." Charles, the guy who seemed to be in charge, assured us.

I wanted to wait around for them to bring Jimmy down. They were insistent that I go to Lions Gate Hospital to get checked out. It was mandatory. They claimed I had a head injury, hypothermia, and some incoherence, which must be examined and assessed. More protocols. Delia agreed with the authorities and convinced me that it was the right thing to do. She would stay and wait for Jimmy.

Thus, the waiting began all over. The people at the hospital were nice. They did x-rays or some sort of brain scan on my head, took blood, and did some neurological tests. I checked out okay and they let my mum take me home. We climbed into mum's two seater Smart Car, which was made by Mercedes, but was her version of "the people's car" ala Volkswagen bugs in the 1960's. I explained that I wanted to go back to the mountain. I wanted to know what was going on with the search. Which way did Jimmy go, and where did he end up? Where is Jim?

Mum's cell phone started ringing and interrupted our discussion. Reading the call display mum said, "It's Delia." Mum tried to contain her excitement. She was hoping for good news, but Delia told her there was still no news.

All I could hear was mum saying lots of "yes dear" and "ohmigoodness dear." And finally, "Yes, Delia, will you please explain that to Gerry because he is demanding I return him back to the mountain to wait with you for Jimmy."

Passing me her cell phone mum mouths, "Do not upset her!"

Bummer, because that had been my plan, I thought this would be a good time to cause a commotion. Get mad and tell them to search harder. "Hi Delia, no sign of Jim yet?" I asked. "How about the helicopters?"

She explained that they were calling off the search for tonight because of the darkness and danger to the searchers in the steep terrain. They had covered a grid search starting where I last saw him, but to no avail. She "will keep me posted."

Mum was intent on taking me back to the family home to convalesce. I wanted to go home to my place. I pleaded that I was fine and that I am twenty-six years old, not a child anymore. It was no us arguing; mum overruled any of my suggestions.

Mrs. Swanson and Jimmy's other sister, Colleen, were waiting at my parents' place in Dunbar. We all had some hugs, exchanged some pleasantries, and chit chatted for a while. Although they had heard my side of the story from Delia and the search authorities, it was comforting for them to hear from me, first hand and directly.

Colleen reached out, stroked my back saying, "Hey Gerry, sorry about all this. We understand. Wish Jimmy had stayed with you, but we know Jimmy, eh. He has to do things his way."

Dr. Swanson telephoned for the Dunbar update and he suggested they disengage for the evening. This time nobody gave him any opposition. They passed the telephone around, as that was the family custom. I was last on the line.

"Gerald, don't you worry young man," Dr. Swanson said with his firm reassuring baritone voice, "They will find Jimmy. It is just a matter of time. These things happen all the time. He is up there somewhere and they will find him."

"Yes, Uncle Russell," I replied, "I just hope they find him soon. It is so cold up there at night time, and he is only wearing a t-shirt and shorts."

"I know Gerald. He is a tough customer. Don't you worry. He will be okay. It is just a matter of time."

Later on that night, lying in my old childhood bedroom, I could not sleep at all. I was tossing and turning and I could only wonder where Jimmy was sleeping. He must be so cold, tired, and hungry.

At first light I got dressed, descended the stairs to find my mum making muffins in the kitchen. She knew I would be going back up the mountain as soon as I could. She did not want me to arrive empty handed. Mum thought the muffins would be "nice for the people working so hard to find Jimmy."

My dad is a dentist, but he is also a collector of fine motorcycles. He was happy when mum got the little micro car because it made more room in the garage for his bike collection. I kick started the old 1975 BMW, put the muffins in the saddlebags, and took off for Grouse Mountain.

Delia's little white Mini Cooper convertible was already in the parking lot when I arrived. We met with some of the search officials and they updated us on their plans and search strategies. We did this day after day, and still no sign of Jimmy. At first, there were a lot of family and friends who showed up to offer support, and with time the numbers started to dwindle. We were not allowed to do any searching in the high ground because it was too dangerous and they worried about losing more people.

Delia and I carpooled. She worked as an Associate Professor in the Chemistry Department at the University of British Columbia. This was her research term and she had the time to spend with me. No teaching duties required this term. She had been awarded a large grant to do research concerned with enzyme substrate protein decay in conjunction with cancer causing peptides. I listened intently, understanding very little, but hey, no one ever said accounting was all that riveting or interesting to normal people, either.

Delia and I began to spend a lot of time together: breakfast, lunch, and dinner. We would not give up hope. We all just expected that they would find Jimmy. He had to be holed up somewhere. Everyday we thought this would be the day. It was tough and we were frustrated. We were included in the discussions and deliberations of the search team, but the team's numbers and resources quickly started to diminish. They were great, but realistic, too.

Eventually the endeavour changed from a search to a recovery mission. At first we protested vehemently, but realistically, we understood. It was not what we wanted, but we understood.

Then the west coast Vancouver fall seasonal rains came. The rains were a torrential deluge and they poured full force for two weeks straight. Actually, it was not unusual weather for this time of year, but it was brutal. It was always dark, too. It was the kind of Vancouver day that causes Seasonal Affective Disorder Syndrome (SADS). The kind of day where you open the curtains and due to the laws of physics all the light gets sucked out and the room gets darker. It was the kind of day where the clouds pack up against the mountains and produce a low ceiling, which makes you feel claustrophobic. The weather was depressing. I was depressed.

And then it happened. I had just picked up Delia at her Kitsilano condominium. We were going to get morning coffee and make plans for the day. While we were discussing the itinerary her cell phone rang.

"Hello, yes this is Dr. Delia Swanson speaking." She responded with a formal tone to the caller.

Her face said all I needed to know. They found Jimmy.

"Yes, thank you, I am sorry, too. Yes, of course, I would prefer to tell my parents personally. Yes, Gerald Westonmeyer is with me right now, and I will tell him."

We always knew this day was going to come, we just did not know when it would arrive. It turns out that Jimmy had fallen off a cliff that night walking in the dark. He either slipped and fell or just walked right off because of the darkness. Somehow his body had gotten entangled in the underbrush and debris. They had searched the area, twice, and saw nothing. The heavy rains caused a mudslide and when that happened Jimmy's body tumbled down to the valley area where they found him at last.

It was a positive identification. Delia and I went to the area where they found Jimmy with a dozen roses and his photograph. A shrine I guess. It was a tough day and it took a heavy toll on us. We stood around for a while, talked, cried, and decided to go home when the rain got heavier.

Pulling up to Delia's condo, she asked, "Do you want to come up?"

"Sure, it's getting late though, and don't forget, we have the big extended family meeting tomorrow."

"It will be okay Gerry. I can deal with the folks. Besides, we deserve a drink tonight."

Throwing a funeral takes planning - lot of planning. Organization, invitations, notifications, funeral homes, and eulogies are all requiring attention and details. Clearly, there were a lot of things to discuss. I am not a funeral person, but Delia explained the cultural importance, and healing aspects for the family. I wanted to argue about the healing part, but took the high road. Closure, I am not sure about the closure concept, but some seemed to think that way. Show the family flag. Show the world something. A united front, I guess. I was just so thankful the open casket viewing service situation had been negated early in the preliminary telephone discussions.

As a young kid I remember my grandmother had an open casket funeral and I attended. That was a big mistake; I was traumatized for years, still am. Whose idea was that? It did not even look like her in the wooden box. People were lined up touching her hands. Some even kissed her goodbye. Everyone was crying.

I was an only child, so my family constellation has limitations. Jimmy was the youngest in his family. And even at twenty-seven years of age, he was always the baby of the family. Delia was the oldest, first born, and Colleen the middle child.

Delia's corner condo was in Kitsilano at the foot of Trafalgar Street with a south and west facing view of False Creek, the Burrard Street Bridge and beyond to English Bay. Her taste in décor was neo-modern with a nice touch of wood and leather furniture. Clearly, Delia is a plant person with all sorts of foliage and colour catching sunrays. She had oil paintings and lithographs hung on the walls. A baby grand piano occupied the area that was intended for a dining room.

"What do you prefer?" Delia called from the kitchen, "red or white wine. Or, I have beer if you would like."

"I like white wine, thanks."

Delia poured a lovely glass of white wine. She told me the name, but it meant nothing. It was from Australia. I know little about wine, other than too much red gives me a hangover headache.

Raising her glass, Delia said, "Gerry, I just want to say thank you. These past few weeks have been difficult and you have been my Rock of Gibraltar. Especially today, I do not know what I would have done if you were not there giving me an arm to hold on to and a shoulder to cry on."

I burst back into tears. Spilling the wine and blubbering, "Delia, if only I had made him stay put with me, or if we never went in the first place, this would never have happened. I am so sorry. I am just so sorry!"

She put the glasses down on the coffee table, took me in her arms, rocking, and softly saying, "Its okay, its okay, don't cry, its okay."

I felt so bad. It was over now. Jimmy was really gone. And now his sister was holding me to her breast saying it was okay. It did not feel okay, but Delia felt good. She was so soft and smelled fragrant and fine. Truth was I wouldn't be here if it wasn't for her. She called in the searchers for help. She has been my rock. She had saved me. I liked it when she held my arm.

"I should be thanking you," I whispered. "You were the one who dealt with the media, police, and search parties. Not to mention our respective parents."

"No way man, were you their every step of the way? Yes." she said with a firm squeeze, kissing me on the forehead. "I could not have got through this without you!"

Delia poured me a fresh glass of wine and we toasted.

"Cheers." We raised glasses, clinked, and I took a swig. It tasted good, fruity, and oh so smooth. We finished that first bottle way too fast.

"Gerry, I must excuse myself. I have got to go to the bathroom to take my contact lens out. My eyes are killing me."

"Yeah, yes, sure, Delia," I replied, "but, hey, I should probably shove off and get going home, eh. Tomorrow is going to be another tough day with a lot of family deliberations and discussions."

"No, not yet, can you stay a couple more minutes? I will just be a minute."

"Yes, sure, no problem, my pleasure," I said smiling while she walked down the hall. Its funny, I have known Delia all my life, but I did not know she wore contact lens. When did that happen?

A couple of minutes later she emerged wearing tortoise shell eye glasses, her long black hair was pulled back into a pony tail, and she had changed clothes into a white t-shirt and grey yoga pants. Walking into the kitchen she called out, "So what's it going to be boy, open another bottle of wine, or would you like a cup of decaf?"

I got off the couch, walking towards her past the kitchen counter and said, "Oh my, don't you look sexy?"

"Oh yeah, you think so mister," she said with a big smile.

"Yes, indeed I do," and for some reason, maybe it was the wine, or maybe all the stress from these past weeks, I do not know, I grabbed her by the waist, pulled her towards me and planted a firm kiss on her freshly washed lips. It was a firm kiss, not a cousinly peck type kiss, a serious kiss. The next thing I knew I was putting my tongue in her mouth.

Delia responded by placing her hands under my shirt and pulling it off. We tumbled out of the kitchen onto the floor. First, the tortoise shell eyeglasses came off, followed by the t-shirt, beige bra and yoga pants. We made love. It was passionate, sweaty, and oh so delectable.

She straddled and sat on me, moaning and we plunged together, "Yes, yes, oh, yes," she screamed, "I want you to fuck me!"

And I did.

We lay on the floor for a little while catching our breath. Delia smiled and whispered, "Lets change venues, my bed is a little more comfortable than this hardwood floor."

Indeed her bedroom was neat and tidy. The lavender coloured pastel sheets on the sleigh bed were soft with a higher thread count than I had ever lain upon.

We made love, again, and again. I did not fall a sleep for a long while, but Delia did. She was sound a sleep and I watched her softly breathing. A full moon lit up the bedroom with a low level of light, but it was bright enough to see Delia clearly.

Blame it on the full moon. I know hospital emergency rooms report high levels of activity on a full moon. The cops say they are overworked on a full moon. And here I was with the moonlight shining on Delia. She looked so beautiful, sound a sleep, and peaceful. Her breasts a perfect pear shape, stomach flat and firm, her black pubic hair waxed and coiffed, but all matted and sticky now from love making.

Morning came too soon. I had drifted off into a light sleep of semi consciousness. I felt Delia stirring, opened my eyes to see her beginning to waken.

"Hi, how you doing?" she said with a smile, pulling me closer. We kissed, snuggled, and agreed that we needed to rise and get on with the day. It was already eight o'clock and we had a couple of hours to get ready to meet the families.

I drove home in a light drizzle. Showered, shaved, drank some strong coffee, and tried to pull myself together thinking out loud, "Uh oh, what have I done?"

You cannot have sex with your cousin. I think it is probably illegal. Anthropologically, morally, medically, it is wrong. We would have genetically mutated children. This was not Alabama or the Ozarks. You cannot have sex with your cousin. But, I did.

In the middle of the night we had discussed safe sex and the possible pregnancy issue. Of course, that barn door was wide open because we had already made love a few times at that point. However, Delia told me to rest assured as she was on the pill. She explained the pill was not really intended as much for pregnancy prevention as it helped curtail cramping aches and pains from the menstrual cycle. PMS I guess. Delia was not promiscuous. Rather, a dedicated professor engaged and committed to her research in the laboratory. She said there had not been much time the past few years for dating or boyfriends.

Actually, I knew that, she was family; she was Jimmy's older sister, and he used to talk about both his sisters all the time.

Normally, I am not a dawdler. I get things done, arrive punctually, and I am reliable. Today I was slower off the mark. I was the last of the expected parties get to the Swanson's house. They were all waiting for my arrival, and of course my tardiness caused undue anxiety for my mum. I felt bad about that, but mind you, I was feeling bad about a bunch of things. Dad did not come due to a dental emergency. Besides, he is no good at these things.

"Hi honey, how you doing?" my aunt greeted me with a hug and a kiss on the cheek, ushering me through the door down the hall to the dining room table where everyone was gathered, drinking tea with muffins.

Colleen jumped up from the table and offered a big firm hug. She whispered in my ear, "Thanks for coming, Gerry, I know you are having a tough time. We all are."

In my mind I thought, "Colleen you do not know the half of it." We did hugs and cheek pecking kisses around the table. Delia gave me an extra squeeze when it was her turn. And my mum began to cry with my hug. This was a tough time.

The funeral service was five days later at Shaughnessy United Church at Thirty Third Avenue and Granville Street. It ended up being a big funeral. I do not know how many people were actually there, but it was a couple hundred and more. A lot of people knew Jimmy. A lot of people were connected to the Swanson family. Guess we advertised the service in the newspapers obituary columns, which brought out more people than we originally expected. "In lieu of flowers please make a donation to Search and Rescue."

Mr. Sidhu was there. He was so old, walking with a stick now, he grasped me by the hand, spitting while he spoke, and said, "Live till you live, man."

Jimmy's old girlfriend, Breanne, from Pouce Coupe—a suburb of Dawson Creek—sat in row three. She cried and wailed throughout the service. And Jimmy said she hated him.

The eulogies were nice. People said such nice things about Jimmy. Both sisters got up front to the pulpit said how much they would miss his humour, hijinks, jokes, and the way Jimmy could make you feel.

Then it was my turn. It was expected that I would say something. It was the right thing to do. The family gave me many opportunities to opt out and not say anything, just sit in the church pew, show the family flag, and be there. It was well acknowledged that this had been a stressful period, and maybe I was not ready for public speaking. Everyone would understand. But, I was the last person to see Jimmy alive. I was his cousin, best friend, confidant, wingman, and I needed to say something. Of course, I could not say I had sex six times with his sister. I had a written a script on an index card stuffed into the pocket of the new black suit my dad had purchased and insisted on my wearing. The black suit was appropriate for the occasion, however, I felt like a fraud wearing the funeral costume, black-suited, white lapel rose, and going through the motions. I felt as though I had been on autopilot, cruise control, and standing up in front of all those people I stuck to the script, but I also spoke from the heart. I said how sorry I felt about losing Jimmy. I publicly apologized for my part in losing Jimmy. I asked forgiveness. I ended by putting my right hand over my heart, kissing the finger tips of my left hand and pointing to the sky, I said, "I love you Jim, wherever you are now, be in peace."

I walked down the church stairs and out the door. That was it, I was done, and all the closure they told me the funeral service would bring did not materialize, and still has not. My therapist encouraged me by saying, "Give it time. Gerald, these things take time."

Delia and I met in neutral territories a few of times to "talk." We could not adequately talk on the telephone, but restaurants and coffee shops were not satisfactory either. We agreed that we had not made a "mistake" and Delia encouraged me to think of the "beauty of our love for each other."

"I lost one cousin when we lost Jimmy, and now I will lose you too," I explained to Delia.

"No, you will never lose me, Gerry," Delia whispered in my ear as we hugged, stopping momentarily while walking along Jericho Beach to where our cars were parked at Locarno Beach, "I will always be in your heart." It sounded corny, but it would have to suffice, it was the best she could do, and I knew it.

I saw Delia one last time when my parents and I went with Jimmy's family to cast his ashes to the wind and sea in the middle of Howe Sound. This was one of the family's favourite sailing destinations.

I took an initial leave of absence from the firm. I went traveling for a while, ended up settling in Australia for two years, and then another year in India before returning to Vancouver.

Although I had been invited to Delia's wedding, I did not attend. I invoked the "it is too far to go" clause and everyone understood. She married a cancer surgeon, and from all reports he is a "heckuva guy." I should expect nothing less. They have a baby boy and his name is James.

Recently, I went back to accounting. The old firm had changed remarkably, but still the same in many respects. A lot of the same people were still working for the firm and a sprinkling of new associates, too. It was okay. The pay was fine and I liked being back. I was happy they took me back.

I trained, conditioned and got into good physical shape. I often run up the Grouse Grind after work and on weekends. My current personal best time is fifty-four minutes. It is a good time, certainly much faster than years ago. I am still working on improvements. During the 2015 election campaign Justin Trudeau completed the Grouse Grind in fifty-five minutes.

I think about Jimmy all the time, at least a dozen times a day. I think about Delia, too. Time has not made much of a difference, and maybe it never will. I miss them.

I am thankful for all that my crazy cousins have given me. I am the better for their love. It is good and I am moving on. "Live till you live."

LEFT BEHIND
―――――――――――

After Jimmy Swanson's funeral I went on a big, big bender. Michael claims it was a memorial, *not* a funeral. I do not know the death distinction, but I have learned the difference between Johnny Walker Red label scotch and Johnny Walker Black. Now that distinction is important. Johnny Walker Blue was never ever in play.

Everyone says I am just depressed. No way, screw that, it makes no sense. One of my best friends fell off Grouse Mountain and *died*. I have not gone to work for three weeks. I am not going anywhere anyway; I am treading water, running on the spot on this treadmill called life. Depressed, nah, not me.

Evidently, Gerald Westonmeyer, Jimmy's cousin and best friend, took off for India. Michael says Australia, but who cares anyway, they are both long gone now. People are saying Gerald had an affair with one of Jimmy's sisters. All you need is love. He should know, John Lennon said so.

Cognitively, I know I am having some mental problems. My mind is a mess. I'm a bit confused. Of course, look at all these empty booze bottles lying around, but another issue: I think I might have had some sex with Breanne from Pouce Coupe—a suburb of Dawson Creek. On the other hand, I am hoping that it was a dream.

Everybody dreams about sex with Breanne from Pouce Coupe and that is normal. I do remember she came over to my place after the wake/celebration of life-thing. I remember we started drinking some wine, she brought pot, and I remember switching to scotch whiskey after the wine was done. She started crying because Jimmy always said, "*Rule number one* when drinking: Do not mix your grapes and grains." As a gentleman, I had to comfort her with a hug and a bit of a back rub. I bet this sort of thing happens all the time around these cultural ceremonies. One thing leads to another. At first you are offering a shoulder to cry on, next thing you know it is morning and you are wondering what happened the night before. Everything is fuzzy and my head hurts.

The unfamiliar empty box of fancy condoms makes me think it may have happened. I buy generic cheap condoms. These definitely look like the kind Breanne would buy. She is stylish. I just do not remember all the circumstances or her leaving. The bad news is my long-term memory is intact. I can remember everything that brought me into this state. It is my short-term memory that is a blur. Blame it on the booze. Blame it on Jimmy's death. Blame it on my faulty memory. Blame it on my stupid boss. Blame it on boredom. Don't blame me.

Grandma got demented and had memory issues. Often I would bring fresh vegetables and milk to her house. She would put them in the fridge and talk to me about things that happened decades ago. Five minutes would go by and she would ask, "Craig, did you bring carrots?" She had commented on how nice they looked five minutes ago but then could not remember. What a piss-off, eh? You spend your whole life making memories only to lose them.

My mum recently retired. She took early retirement, freedom fifty-five, or some new mantra. After dad's death she took on widow status with an unmitigated vigour that we had not expected. She was assertive, not aggressive, and she is quick to point out the significant difference between the two. The newly appointed principal at Prince of Wales gave mum some crappy courses to teach so she quit. The preferred polite term is retirement, but really, c'mon, it is the same as quitting.

Mum moved to Mayne Island. She sold our old family home for big bucks and she was gone. My sister seemed to take it well. Sis is always a glass half full person anyway. "Craig, aren't you just so proud of mum? The way she has picked herself up and put herself together is really awesome. I sure miss dad," Debbie would say.

Amy Bains, my best friend Michael's girlfriend since high school, called to blast me both barrels. The thing about telephone messages you see on television, it is different than real life. On television you can hear the message while you stare at the telephone. In real life you have to listen to the phone ring three times, look at call display, and decide whether to answer, look to see if they left a message when you did not answer, then punch in your code to listen to the message. It is way too complicated in real life.

"Davidsen you dork!" Amy began, "I do not understand you. Michael says you have not gone to work in over *three* weeks. He is worried ill about you. His problems are my problems. We will not stand by and let you waste away. And what is this stuff I am hearing about you and Breanne? If you do not call me back in the next few hours and assure me that you are going to surface, get back to work and get yourself together, I am coming over with Debbie. We are going to have an *intervention.*"

Talking to myself, "Sorry, Amy, but aren't interventions suppose to be a surprise? Telling, or threatening me in advance sort of defeats the purpose." But, nonetheless, I did not want to deal with Debbie and Amy. I did not want an intervention. Clearly, it was time to get out of town. I drove to Tsawwassen, climbed onto the Queen of Nanaimo ferry to visit mum on Mayne Island. It was the only nondrastic thing I could think of. Besides, visiting mum on Mayne seemed like a good way to get myself together or regroup or something else other than going back to the firm and "the working lifestyle."

It was actually a nice winter's day with a blue sky and sunshine providing a modest level of warmth. The ferry was not crowded and I stood outside on the deck watching both the sun and mainland fade in the distance. Folklore has it that Mark Twain said the worst winter he ever spent was one summer in San Francisco. I am not a winter person, although I am still trying. Jimmy said he liked all the seasons the same amount. He did not have a favourite season. Jimmy was good that way.

Mum's prowess as an historian was heavily inflicted on me the last time I visited. At first I made like her archival depictions were too boring to endure, but I actually found it interesting? Her new home on Mayne Island is located in the Southern Gulf Island archipelago where Captain George Vancouver had camped back in 1794. This was documented and authenticated by a coin found by early settlers that had been left behind at Georgina Point by someone on Vancouver's ship. Mayne Island was named after Lieutenant Richard Mayne, one of the Royal Navy surveyors in 1852.

Mum's cottage was on the edge of Miner's Bay where the Caribou gold rush settlers stayed on their way through Active Pass in the mid 1800s. It was a rough and tumble time. The Springwater Lodge was built in 1892 as well as the police constable's residence, magistrate's court and lockup. Henry Scotty Georgeson was the island's first lighthouse keeper and he recorded the last lockup entry in January 1912. Victoria and Vancouver took over the administration of the law.

Daydreaming I remembered when Jimmy got arrested last year because he had a bad spasm about parking meters. He got into a fight with civic workers, and it all went south. His lawyer negotiated an out of court settlement. It was idiotic from beginning to end.

Standing on the outside top promenade deck as the ferry chugged its way through Active Pass between Galiano and Mayne Island, I could see mum's cottage on the edge of Miner's Bay. Without binoculars I could not distinguish what kind of action was happening in the front of her place, but it made me smile to see some buzzing around mum's beachfront home. I was really looking forward to seeing her again. Her recalcitrance was admirable.

The ferry docked, I finally disembarked and began driving along the narrow winding rural island road to mum's place. I stopped first at the General Trading Post and Liquor Store to purchase the best bottle of champagne that Edith the proprietress had in stock for sale. I also acquired a small mickey size Johnny Walker Red, too.

Mum had become an avid kayaker. When I arrived at her house she and her kayak coach, Leslie, had all the gear spread out on the beach in front of her house. They had colourful paddles, an ocean wave spray skirt to cover the cockpit, throw ropes, bailing pump, life jackets, peanut sponges, laminated maps, plastic stow bags, and an assortment of other items that had no meaning to me.

Mum's kayak was a bright yellow kevlar construction and only weighed seventeen kilograms so she could transport and portage it solo. Shows you what I know, I had thought kevlar was used for cops' bullet proof vests, but it turns out to be a lightweight strong material for kayaks, too.

I had gone kayaking before at Jericho Beach with Jimmy and Gerald so I had some experience. Of course, those two practiced the Inuit roll, but I would not consent to purposely dumping the kayak and rolling over. I hate hypothermia.

Upon arrival it was big hugs all around. Mum was surprised, but certainly happy to see her "baby boy" and although I am twenty-seven years old, I will always be her baby. I had met Leslie before as well as some of mum's other new friends. Mum was so good that way, gregarious and good at making friends. I am the antithesis, but still trying.

We walked over to the Springwater Lodge for a beer followed by dinner. It was just like that old television show where everybody knows your name and they are always glad you came. We settled in a nice little corner table with a view of Active Pass and the parade of gigantic ferries plying people back and forth from Victoria to Vancouver.

"So, how you doing Craig?" mum asked. "Debbie thinks you are depressed. I told her I am depressed too. Just thinking about Jimmy is pretty depressing, eh?"

"Are you really depressed mum, or are you just saying that to make me feel better?"

"Oh I wish I could make you feel better, Craig. I wish your dad were still here. I wish Jimmy was with still us. Those fun loving crazy guys always go first and leave us behind. It sucks, I know, but what can I do about my depression, or yours? Life goes on, one way or another, or not. The sunrises, a few things happen, the sunsets, and the day is done. The next day we do it again. I don't know why we are here or what we should do with our time here. It's the life we live and that's just how it goes, I guess. You want another beer?"

"Sure."

And as Jimmy would say, "that was that." We had another couple of beers and called it a night. It was time to disengage, say our goodnights to the gang, and waddle homewards. When we got out of the Springwater and started strolling it was brisk and black. Mum, as a good Girl Guide Scout, had two flashlights to aide our travel along the shortcut trail to her beach house. There aren't any streetlights to illuminate the path and clouds shrouded the moon. It was great. I had enjoyed the dinner, the beers, the evening stroll home, and mum's therapeutic candour. Mum was not so mushy, but she soldiered on, one foot in front of the other, one day at a time. Debbie was right, mum was cool, and she had put herself together, picked up the pieces, and was doing well in her new lifestyle. I was proud of her.

The cottage was still quite cozy when we returned. Mum had stoked the airtight wood stove with some sweet smelling fir firewood before leaving and it was still burning with a good glow. Mum had mastered the art of burning wood efficiently and effectively. It gave a nice comfortable source of warmth.

"Nightcap?" I asked.

"No thanks dear," she replied, "I have to get up early tomorrow, but you help yourself. I'm going to call it a night."

I rummaged through the liquor cabinet and pulled out a lovely bottle of Remy Martin Cognac. I poured a modest to healthy glass and settled into the leather sofa by the fire. The cognac was warming and smooth down the gullet. I was relaxed. Of course, I nodded off on the couch and woke up around three a.m. with a startle. It took me a minute to get oriented. I cleaned things up and changed venue to the back bedroom. I fell back into a deep sleep and stayed that way until almost noon the next day.

Mum works as a volunteer at the Mayne Island Public Library. She is still part of the hardcopy generation that loves to hold books in her hands. She started going quasi-digital, but hangs on to the old hardcopy. However, having said that, I like her handwritten notes way better than an email or text message.

Mum's colourful note was left on the kitchen counter in prominent view, anchored by an upside-down cut up grapefruit and aspirin bottle. "Craig, hope you had a good sleep, help yourself to the coffee and breakfast. I will be at the library until five this afternoon. See you later. Love mum xoxox." And her version of a happy face logo, too.

Mum gets coffee from McDougall's Farm Gate Store. The coffee is eco friendly, double organic, shade grown, or fair trade, I do not know exactly which stripe is most prominent in the purchase, but it is indeed good coffee. I was on my second cup of coffee, and just like Gordon Lightfoot, I still could not face the day. So what the hell, I added some of last night's brandy into the coffee. The Italians call it correcto coffee. Yes, some correcting is definitely needed here.

Mum was in training. Historically, mum was always in training for something. Whether it was the Vancouver Half Marathon, Sun Run, False Creek Dragon Boat Races, or tap dancing with the Mayne Island Tap Dancers May Queen festivities, mum was always in training for something. This time she was in training for this spring's upcoming kayak trip to Tumbo Island with her kayak club.

Mum's maps and brochures were scattered on her desk by the window nook overlooking Active Pass and Prevost Island. The photographs of Tumbo Island looked attractive. Their plan was to do the four-hour paddle from Mayne Island to Tumbo, setup a campsite, and explore the islands for two days and then paddle back home. It sounded ambitious to me, but it was an adventure. Mum was always up for an adventure. She is good that way.

Mum's notes and travel plans show that Tumbo Island has a long history. The Coast Salish First Nations Indians did a lot of salmon fishing off Tumbo. Tumbo Island got the name from its tombolo shape. It turns out that a tombolo is a sandbar, which juts outward and connects one island to another island, especially at low tide. The most famous tombolo that I remember reading about is Chappaquiddick Island, at Martha's Vineyard in Massachusetts. One of the Kennedy clan had a mishap there, can't remember which one, but who cares these days anyway, eh?

I went outside, sat on the deck, finished my coffee and wandered around the place. Checking out mum's new kayak, I decided to get myself together and take it out for a paddle. Last summer mum and I had gone paddling and I knew that Bennett Bay was a good place to launch and explore the northeastern shores of Mayne and the outer islands.

It was still fairly early in the afternoon, around two o'clock, when I pushed off from the sandy beach at Bennett Bay. The sun was shining and the sea was so clear. I could see the sandy bottom with crabs crawling in between the Campbell Point Peninsula and Georgeson Island. Evidently, in the winter months the sea is clear because there is not as much plankton and algae in the water or something to that effect. That is why scuba divers prefer winter dives. Regardless of the biological conjectures, it was just beautiful to skim the sea's surface so effortlessly. I kept going past Georgeson Passage towards the Belle Chain Islets where the sea lions were engaged in their choir practice. I joined in with my rendition of Louis Armstrong's "What a Wonderful World." As I got closer to one of the Belle Islets I could see the bottom again and had to be careful not to scratch mum's new kayak on the sudden ridge of rocks just under the surface. A couple of barking bulls rolled into the water as I approached and although I was sure that it meant nothing as far as danger was concerned, prudence persuaded me that moving away quickly was a good idea. I paddled furiously and got some distance between the islets and sea lions with their mating.

Trouble was now the water was getting rougher and I was getting too far from shore so I pulled hard on the rudder and headed back towards the shoreline. Once I got out of the open ocean and in between Samuel and Curlew Islands the wind was gone and the water was nice and calm.

At first I was not frightened. Cruising past Curlew Island spilling into Horton Bay, I saw what looked like an albino seal making weird noises. Following the seal through Robson Channel where it narrows, I then heard another weird noise. It was a lot like the sound of water rushing over rocks. It sort of sounded a lot like laughing river rapids, but I was in the ocean. Little did I know, but this sound of water running indicated the tide had turned. I had made a mistake. I had not paid attention to the turning tide. I had stayed out too long, gone too far down the narrow channel and was now quickly being pushed way down the channel back into the open ocean towards the Americans, too. Picking a visual marker on Lizard Island's shore I paddled furiously, but it was hopeless. I was floating the wrong way. The winter current was five knots too strong. I tried not to panic; however, darkness was now starting to fall fast. Unlike summertime there is little to no marine traffic available to help in winter. Now, I knew I was in a little bit of trouble.

Statistically, I knew hospital emergency wards and police stations both report full moon frenzies. Strong tides are correlated to full moons. I should have known better. I remember seeing the "Tide and Current Tables" on mum's desk. What was I thinking? Why didn't I check the tide table? Why wasn't I paying attention? Of course, everyone says that. Yes, hindsight is so clear. However, I should have known the gravity of turning tides and subsequent current flow was going to be way too much for me to handle. Business people and politicians say the same thing about turning tides in their endeavours. Paying attention is hard when you are cruising along doing your thing to your own tune. All of a sudden the tide turns, you missed the signs, and now the current is quickly surging in the opposite direction to where I wanted to go. This is accentuated in a narrow island channel.

Paddling against the fast flowing current was futile. I was in the middle of the channel when I realized that this was where water flow is fastest. I had selected the middle of the channel because it was deep and the shoreline was too rocky. I had to pick a place on the shore to land and stop my progress. I knew paddling over to Lizard Island would not be helpful because it was smaller and it looked even more deserted. At least Mayne Island has some summer cottages sporadically placed along the shore. Too bad that I had not seen a cottage for the past while, but nevertheless I had to find a place to beach the kayak.

The shoreline was rocky with Arbutus trees jutting out at sharp angles. It did not matter; I had to get to shore. I picked a spot where I saw an opening, but before I could get close enough the current pushed me past the spot and down through the rocky cliff face. I decided to open the spray skirt and reach behind the seat where the towrope was stored. My plan was to lasso a tree to at least stop my progress and then figure out a new plan because it was starting to get dark.

Although I knew opening the spray skirt would make me vulnerable to getting swamped, I had no choice; I needed the rope that was stowed behind the cockpit's seat. I fumbled with the elastic cord, but I managed to get it open and reach behind for the rope. While I was retrieving the rope the kayak was swept into a swirling eddy, which spun the bow around, and I was now facing the wrong way. Panicking, I put the paddle down to correct the spin, but that did not help. It caused me to lean too far and before I could correct the lean I dumped.

It was not a sudden and startling flip; it was a slow roll into the freezing cold winter water. Unlike folklore, where your life flashes before your eyes just before death, I experienced a déjà vu. Some years ago when I was riding my motorcycle down Victoria's Quadra Street, (the roads there hardly never freeze over, but on that day there was frost coating the road). I took a curve and I could feel the bike sliding out from under me. I desperately tried to keep it upright. One of the mantras from motorcycle training school was "Never lay your bike down, never give up." Once the bike was down, you were done; you no longer had any control, and would have to suffer the consequences of others actions, like getting run over. As my bike was sliding - and it seemed like a slow slide, but it was not - I could see the stopped truck ahead of me at a red light intersection. I thought that was that, and this was a done deal, I would surely die. However, the truck started to move forward and my sliding bike stopped. The Volvo behind me swerved and I lived to dump mum's kayak just off Mayne Island some years later.

Unlike Jimmy and Gerald, I did not practice the Inuit roll, back at Jericho Beach when we took some kayak training. However, even if I did know how to do an Inuit kayak roll it would not have helped me because it only works with a sealed cockpit. To my detriment, I had undone the spray skirt to get the rope from behind the seat to lasso a rock or tree branch to stop my progress going the wrong way south.

The water was painfully freezing cold and I struggled to get out of the kayak. Once I was free from the cockpit I swam to the surface and started grappling for the paddle before it floated away, and most importantly, the swamped kayak. With a rush of adrenaline and fear I kicked like crazy and pushed the boat towards the shore. At least now I had retrieved the towrope because the pouch that contains the rope floats. As soon as I could touch the bottom I knew I would not drown. I may die from hypothermia, but I was not going fill my lungs with cold salty water.

As soon as I could stand on both feet I tried to upright the kayak and empty out the water. I got to the rocky shore, sat on a rock and started to shiver. I knew I could not stay there long as darkness was falling fast. I realized the current was not as swift along the shallow water by the shore. I tied the rope around my waist and onto the bow. I started to slush and walk along the shore. If I could only make it through the channel and get close to Horton Bay I would be okay. I was soaking wet, shivering, but still plodding along the shoreline.

I thought about Jimmy Swanson. He undoubtedly experienced the same sort of situation as he tromped along the top of Grouse Mountain before falling to his death. Was he lonely? Was he scared?

Was he repentant? I know for sure he was not this cold. He must have felt terrible. He must have been so sad.

Everyone says if Jimmy just stayed still like Gerald, he would have been rescued. Staying still was not an option for me, although I did think about it. If I had waterproof matches I could start a fire, get dry, warm up, and wait for help to arrive. If I had a cell phone I could call for help. I had neither. There was no one around, no one on the water, and no one along the shore. In the summer there are lots of people around. There are many sailboats, outboards, inboards, and a constant parade of marine traffic plying through these channels, but not in the winter.

Now it is getting harder to see where I was going as it is getting progressively darker. If I cannot get through the channel into the mouth of Horton Bay before it is completely dark, I will die for sure. When it gets completely dark I will not be able to see what is in front of me and my progress will stop. Unlike Jimmy, I won't fall to my death, but it will just as disorienting and deadly.

I just kept plodding along the shoreline, dodging Arbutus trees that jutted outwards, rocks, and deep-water pools. Otherwise I was able to tow the kayak and walk along in the shallow water by the shoreline.

Tides flood and ebb. There is also a slack period between the two. I thought I felt some slackening of the current's force, and just as soon as I could get out of this channel I would get back into the kayak and paddle back to safety.

The proverbial light at the end of the tunnel occurred when I could see a light shining from a Horton Bay house in the distance. I could not really judge how much farther I had to go. I was cold and getting disoriented. I still had some distance to go before the mouth of the bay, but I decided to get back in the kayak and start paddling.

My legs felt like rubber. I had been wading for a while and my arms were well rested and ready to work. The current had indeed slackened. I stayed close to the shore where the current was not as strong, but not too close where I could hit a rock. Eventually I exited the channel and was now entering the bay. I had to decide whether to dock and knock on the door of the house with the light on, or paddle through the middle of the bay and push on past Curlew Island through to Bennett Beach where my car was waiting.

After coming this far I decided to just keep going to the car. Who knows whether the house with the light had anyone who could help? Regardless, I had to dry off and get warm. It seemed like getting back to my car was the best bet. I kept paddling, and paddling. I could see more lights shining in homes along Curlew, Bakerview, and Charter Road. It was dark and cold, but I knew where I was and where I was going.

I finally made it back to Bennett Beach. I pulled the kayak up on the sandy shore, sat on a log, and heaved a huge sigh of relief. It was over, finished, and I had actually made it back to where I started. I t was dark and I was cold, but I had dodged a disaster and lived to tell the story. It was a close call, too close for my liking. I was just too stupid for words. It had been a big mistake, but now I was on the other side of the mistake, and it did not matter that much now.

I flung the kayak onto the roof rack, got inside the car and smiled. Prior to setting off to Bennett Bay I had stopped at the Farm Gate Store to pick up a couple of Shanti's muffins. I was going to get three or four, but Don the proprietor and I got into a discussion about Robbie Robertson's song: "The night they drove old Dixie down" with the lyric that says: Just take what you need leave the rest.

I devoured the two muffins that had been patiently waiting on the passenger's seat.

When I drove back to mum's place she had not even really noticed that I was gone for very long, or that there was anything askew. She had not noticed that I had borrowed her kayak. Even though I had been through what I thought was an eternity, it was only seven o'clock in the evening. "Hi dear," I heard her say as I came through the back door, "I'm just getting dinner together. Are you hungry?"

"Yes, sounds great," I replied. "I'm just going to get cleaned up before dinner."

"Okay dear, dinner will be ready soon."

I had a quick shower, changed my clothes, and then sat down for a home cooked meal. "How was the library today, mum?"

"It was busy. We had a lot of new books to process, but it was good. Afterwards, Betty Martin and I went to her place to bake some pies for this weekend's party. I do hope you will still be here for the party, Craig."

"Yes, sure, I will still be here for your party, but I have to get back to Vancouver before I lose my job. Could you please pass me another biscuit?"

"Oh that is a good idea. Did you have a good day today?"

"Yes, it was a good day, thanks." I did not think it was worthwhile to review today's adventure at this point. I did not want to spoil the mood. Tomorrow I will have to check out mum's kayak to see how many scratches and dings were done today, but hey, tomorrow is still a day away. Tonight I am going to enjoy mum's company and let tomorrow take care of itself.

Pouce Coupe Clydesdales

The sorrel Clydesdale horse picked up the pace as the barn in the distance came into sight. Seeing the barn the Clydesdale knew it meant lunch, water, a nice rubdown, and brushing.

I wondered how far in the distance a horse could see. I wondered if horses get depressed. I wondered who said you can never go home again because I agree. After spending eighteen years trying to get out of this place it was disheartening to end up back in Pouce Coupe. I had no choice. I hate hospitals. I mean I really hate hospitals, even more than Pouce Coupe. I don't actually hate Pouce Coupe, because this is where I grew up, where my family lives, and where my roots are, but I would rather be somewhere else, like my "happy place."

Whenever I seemed to be sliding into a less than favourable mood, my recently deceased boyfriend, Jimmy Swanson, used to always say, "Go to your happy place, Breanne." He was a funny guy, a bit crazy, but oh how he could make me laugh. And oh how I prefer laughing to crying. Of course, Joni Mitchell said laughing and crying were the same thing.

When our hospital group therapist suggested we go to our "happy place" I guess I may have over-reacted, or maybe it was a turning point, critical incident, or something less than positive or happy. I know she meant no malice, and she was just doing her job. But, it was too lame to cope with, and I snapped. And if goody-two-shoes, who always sat next to me in-group, had just kept her big mouth shut, things would not have accelerated so fast.

Anthropologically, I think I am third generation Pouce Coupe, but I cannot count well anyway. Of course, my accountant friends are even more creative counters. Is zero a number, or do you start at one? Ten is a place holding number. Nonetheless, I was born in Pouce Coupe, both my ma and papa were born in Pouce Coupe. Grampa, on mother's side, was from Pouce Coupe, but where he was born was always debated. His father, my Great Grampa, was one of the last of the Coureur des bois, or as some say, a voyageur - a French fur trader who sometimes worked for the old Hudson's Bay Company, and HBC means "Here Before Christ." However, he ended up coming here when there was trouble in the east with the Louis Riel rebellion.

"How can a blonde be Métis?" Jimmy would ask.

"Easy, Einstein, Mendel means nothing to you. My great-grandmother was a blonde from Finland. She married a Métis, but that notwithstanding, it is basic genetics. Besides Métis is a French word meaning mixed bloods. Think about it, once you start mixing bloods, genes, and chromosomes, you are going to get blondes, brunettes, and redheads."

"Yes, and everybody knows that blondes have more fun," Jimmy said with a smirk. "Are you having fun, hon?"

I really miss Jimmy. I did have so much fun with him and his crazy accountant friends. That was then, this is now, and one way or another, life goes on, according to my mother's mantra.

Papa was waiting for us at the Dawson Creek Airport. I could see the bright blue van from the window seat of the airplane just before we landed. It was a nice flight, clear weather with spectacular vistas. I bet that guys from the Klondike gold rush wished that they could have easily flown from Vancouver to Dawson Creek. We had just flown over Pouce Coupe, which is a French word meaning cut-off thumb, but there is also archival documentation of a Beaver Indian

Chief named Pooscapee, so the historical debate will rage on with anyone who actually cares. It is not my issue, I have others, and they take greater consideration.

After we entered the airport, Papa spotted us, got up, and ambled along toward us. His big body plodded through the waiting area and we had huge hugs all around. "Hi Papa," I said through watery eyes, "it is good to see you."

"Oh yes my darling, you too," he replied with a strong squeeze.

Papa and I wrestled over who would carry the heaviest pieces of luggage. Mother, reluctant to get involved with our father/daughter drama, had already started making her way out the door. She knew the routine.

It is only a short seven-kilometre drive from the airport to the City of Dawson Creek, and then another sixteen kilometres to Pouce Coupe. The sun was shining and the old homestead seemed to sparkle as we approached. There were horses in the pasture, barking dogs running towards our approaching van, seasoned split wood ready for the shed, crops in the field, and clean laundry on the line. This is where I grew up, my roots ran deep, and I was back home.

The place looked just like I left it, it looked welcoming, but I did *not* want to be here. Actually, I did not want to be anywhere. But be that as it may, given my current circumstances, anywhere is a better place to be.

After Jimmy's funeral, although Craig Davidsen claimed it was technically a memorial, my lower mainland life took a nosedive. Much like a lot of other people in our posse, I always had some latent mental health issues and phobias, but I was functional. I was okay. Of course, I had some eating issues, body image idiosyncrasies, marginal depression, manic maladies on Mondays, and mood swings, but I was basically okay, certainly functional. I had a reasonably good paying job, nice place to live, a wardrobe in process, a busy social life, and I was for the most part basically okay, certainly not dysfunctional. Normal is not the be all and end all anyway. Who do you know that is normal anyway? Maybe diversity is a good thing and abnormalities should be embraced and welcomed.

My crash was inevitable. It didn't hurt that much at first because I did not really see it coming and then when I did it was already too late as I was going down too fast to stop the momentum from forcing the issue. I had lost control and could not retrieve the reins. That wild horse was off at a gallop and I wasn't even hanging on. Of course I was going to fall, when and where were the issues, but I was going to fall. It was inevitable.

Whether they label it as a nervous breakdown, major affective disorder, or just plain going *crazy*. It does not matter all that much what they call it if you're the one they are speaking about. I think the labels help the label makers, but I was out of it anyway, so whatever they put on my hospital chart was of little or no concern to me. The drugs coloured everything a dull brownish blur. I did not know how I got put into the hospital; I just knew I wanted *out*.

St. Paul's Hospital is in downtown Vancouver. Originally, some Catholic Sisters opened the hospital in September 1907. The wing they put me in was built in 1914. The place also had a weird smell, but maybe that was another trick the medications were playing on my brain. My mind was gone, and I really missed it. The smell sucked.

My papa and mother appeared out of nowhere. One minute I am listening to some medical goofball asking goofy questions, and then I am sleeping, dreaming, or drugged up for who knows how long. Then my parents are standing by my bed talking to each other, but they are acting like I cannot comprehend English. Then they are gone, and another goofy guy is putting me through the motions of a mental status exam.

I knew the answers to the mental status exam, but I did not know why he was asking them. My parents were now long gone, however no one was telling me where they went and why. I was groggy and tired all the time. I felt as though I was walking around under water. And I was just so bored.

Even though group therapy sessions seemed stupid, I was just so bored that doing something else other than jigsaw puzzles was better than nothing. I could not really remember all that much about my meltdown so I did not have much to contribute to group. But, be that as it may, I did attend the group because it was mandatory and I had nothing else to do anyway, but it was still so stupid. The group was stupid, the leader was stupid, and all the exercises were even more mentally diminishing. I played along because I had learned while attending university that it was always way easier to swim downstream than work against the current.

After graduating high school, I finally left Pouce Coupe to attend the University of British Columbia. That is where I met Jimmy Swanson. I was working towards a Bachelor of Education degree and he was into business and accounting. We both would go to the same coffee shop first thing in the morning to "coffee-up" to face the day. That is where we first met.

"So, you are getting your degree in bed," Jimmy said jokingly, playing on a Bachelor of Education an acronym. "Degree in bed, get it?" he would say, as if it was an insider joke.

He really was a funny guy, charming, energetic, and he loved to party. Our relationship started slowly and accelerated to a gallop. Jimmy had never heard of Pouce Coupe, but he always talked about coming up to visit and go horseback riding with me. Of course, I said I was gone from Pouce Coupe for good. My time was up and I had moved on to the big smoke.

Graduating from UBC was a happy time. At first I was not planning on attending the convocation ceremonies, but Jimmy, always the prophet and pontificator talked me into it by explaining, "Why do you always think it is all about you? It isn't, it is like a funeral. It provides closure for others. The graduation ceremony allows significant others in your life a chance to take proud photos, dress up, and party. The graduation dinner is like a wake. It is not about you, and it is a cultural passage for others."

Again, Jimmy was correct. My parents and younger sister came to the graduation ceremonies. *They* had a great time, took lots of proud photos, and we had a happy dinner at a fancy Vancouver restaurant. I don't know about the graduation dinner wake thing. I sure did not feel any closure when I attended Jimmy's funeral. Jimmy's wake was weird, too.

Jimmy and I were always breaking up and then making up. It was our routine. It is what we did. When he died we were enduring a relationship hiatus. I really felt bad about that. The last time I saw Jimmy alive I called him a self-centred asshole. The worst part was that he agreed. "Yes, Bree, you are completely correct," he said, and it made me even more angry with him. Forever I will regret that the last time I saw him we parted with angry words.

After graduation, Jimmy and all his accounting friends were on a roll, and life was unfolding as it should. I, on the other hand, was not doing all that well. I had earned a Bachelor of Education degree, but there were no fulltime teaching jobs available in Vancouver. Too many older baby boom teachers and a declining student enrolment coupled with continued government cutbacks, and the system was stagnant. The only way into teaching was as a substitute teacher, or the current politically correct term of "teacher on call," but you were still a substitute teacher. One of my friends lucked out and got a long-term job replacing a teacher who was going on maternity leave. I did do a few short-term stints as a Teacher On Call, but it was too intermittent and my rent was always due at the end of the month. I worked evenings, as a waitress at the Provence Restaurant on Tenth Avenue, but it was not what I wanted to do. Jimmy said I needed a Plan B.

Plan B turned out to be a marketing and advertising job with an upstart Internet yoga clothing and accessories company. Who would have thought that technical yoga apparel would take off and seem so successful? The pay was commensurate with the company's success. Although the pace and all the applause could be a bit stressful, I enjoyed working with the group. It was also helpful to garner a steady pay cheque that met my financial commitments: rent due at month's end.

Of course, it all went down the tubes after Jimmy's death and my subsequent crash. Although I do not remember the details all that much, they drugged the hell out of me, I do remember that I was not paying full attention while driving and I rear ended a big Ford SUV with my beautiful blue 1992 Toyota Tercel—Jimmy always called it the 'turtle'.

Really, it was just a minor accident, just a fender bender, but I started crying, and could not quit. They took me away in an ambulance to St. Paul's Hospital. I remember flailing around a bit, and so they gave me more medication. Whatever type of meds they gave me it was wrong, and too much. I had a seizure. When I woke I had memory loss and the chart at the end of the bed listed me with 'fractational fugue partial amnesia' due to the medication causing some sort of semi-brain damage and dysfunction.

My parents came to Vancouver immediately after the crash. Papa had to get back to Pouce Coupe, but my mother remained in Vancouver for three weeks until my release from the hospital. Plan C was now necessary. It entailed my return to Pouce Coupe to recuperate, recover, regroup, and try to get myself back together.

Equestrian therapy is a popular treatment for autistic people. And even though there was no suggestion that I was autistic, there certainly was a psychotic suggestion riding my back. Consequently, when my mother, and ally, suggested equestrian therapy, all the Vancouver mental health experts concurred, albeit cautiously.

Our family farm still has a lot of horses, not as many as years ago, but still a good number of heads. I have been riding Clydesdale horses all my life. Grampa got me started riding with Clydesdales. Of course, there are jazzier horses that they ride down in Vancouver's Southlands, but Clydesdales are the plodding gentle giants. They originate from Clydesdale, Scotland where they were developed as workhorses. These horses usually weigh around one tonne and grow to almost two metres high. They are not extinct yet, but tractors have replaced Clydesdales on modern farms. Family farms are going extinct, too.

Grampa's farm was anything but modern. He held off acquiring fancy equipment like tractors, combines, and big trucks. He had his Clydesdale horses to work the farm; modern equipment just wasn't necessary. And although as I got older I always thought of Grampa as the epitome of a farming Renaissance man, because he was so wise, patient, and kind. However, the world was turning too fast and more and more there were too many things to try and understand. It was hard for him. My generation never suffers this problem.

"Grampa, how come your house does not have electricity?" I asked. "Mama's house has electricity. It is great. You just open the switch and the light comes on. You could get a refrigerator like mothers. Those things are great and you wouldn't need the icebox anymore."

"Well, Breanne," he would begin, "I don't have things that I don't understand. I don't understand how electricity works, so I don't want it, don't need it. If you don't understand how something works, you shouldn't have it."

That was my Grampa for you. Even though another great left-handed innovator, Benjamin Franklin, had been working with electricity since the mid-seventeen hundreds, and electricity had reached the Pouce Coupe region for many years, Grampa did not understand how it worked, so he did not want it. Of course, papa said it was because he was too stubborn and did not want to spend the money to pay for the line to his farmhouse.

When I was a little girl, there were times when Grampa was theoretically supposed to be babysitting me, but I was always getting underfoot, or to his horror, getting "lost" or out of sight on his farm. If he could not see me, or if he did not know where I was, he would get worried. He had a lovely old chestnut Clydesdale horse that he would put me on. That way he could always see where I was, perched upon the gentle giant's back. "Line of sight" was essential to his comfort zone. I was happy too because we would wander around the place. I could lie down on my tummy, I could move around backwards or sideways, and was very comfortable on the giant back of the Clydesdale. Of course, the only way down was either with Grampa's help or using the ladder on the barn. I would spend hours happily touring the farm's attractions. It was a happy time.

At first I had been really reluctant to return to Pouce Coupe after my release from the hospital. My mother was so good and patient about talking me through the alternatives, and when I realized my alternatives were only exceeded by my lack of health, direction and motivation, I relented. I returned under the auspices of "it is only for a while until I get myself back together." The psychiatrist signed me out.

Of course, everything was easier said than done. One of Grampa's frequent mantras was, "Easy to say, hard to do." As a young child, Pouce Coupe was a great place to be. I loved it. There were so many things to do, so many adventures and places to explore. My Grampa let me ride his horses. Adolescence was not quite as adventuresome. Pouce Coupe was boring. I longed for the excitement, razzmatazz, and bright lights of the big city. Urban migration was normal for most of my graduating group. I wanted to grow up and get out. University and a big city career seemed like the ticket.

Grampa often said, "The grass is always greener on the other side of the hill. If you chase the world Breanne, you will never catch it. You must be patient, let things come to you." Of course, he also said, "Do nothing and no thing will happen? If you want some changes, get out there and do something."

I was sixteen when Grampa died from pneumonia complications and at the old age of seventy-three his time here was over. It was a terribly sad time for those left behind. The funeral was weird, too. His body lay in a fancy casket and it sat in the aisle at the front of the old Anglican Church of Christ during the funeral service. I had been to the old church, which was built in 1932 before, but it was always for weddings and happier occasions. Grampa was buried in our extended family section of the Pouce Coupe cemetery.

Unlike Grampa, Jimmy was cremated. His family spread his ashes in Howe Sound. I was not invited, justifiably so, I guess. I knew it was Jimmy's favourite sailing spot. I had been there with him a dozen times or so. It was always a happy time, even when he played the Captain Bligh role. He could give orders like nobody's business.

Jimmy's memorial service was five days after they had found his body on Grouse Mountain. The service was at Shaughnessy United Church at Thirty Third Avenue and Granville Street. It was a very big event. I do not know how many people were actually there, but it was a couple hundred and more. A lot of people knew Jimmy. A lot of people were connected to the Swanson family. Guess they advertised the service in the newspaper obituary column, which brought out more people than they originally expected. "In lieu of flowers please make a donation to search and rescue." I just cried and cried. The last thing I was going to do, in lieu, was anything but a big donation of tears. Tears, buckets and buckets, but they were not bringing him back. It was an unhappy time.

The sorrel Clydesdale horse made a snorting sound and picked up the pace even faster as the barn in the distance came closer into sight. Whoever said you can never go home was wrong. I did it, and at first I did not want to do it, but in the end it worked out okay. Of course I was out of options anyway, so Pouce Coupe was okay.

Just as Grampa predicted, quit chasing the world let it come to you. It was true. While I was recuperating from my Vancouver crash, Mrs. Geiger, the grade four, five, and six teacher at Pouce Coupe Elementary School, went on a vacation to Cabo San Lucas in Mexico. She met a man, fell in love, and never returned to Pouce Coupe. Consequently, they needed someone with a teaching certificate. I was Breanne on the spot, and the job was mine. It was really good. I loved the kids. I loved the focus. And until I can get myself together, this could be okay.

Craig Davidsen had come to visit. As the horse pulled up to the barn, Craig was waving and smiling from ear to ear. He had learned how to throw a rope over a fence post. He was awfully proud of this accomplishment that had taken three days to master. But, hey, whatever works for you is fine with me. Any accomplishment, no matter how small, is still an accomplishment, and it should be celebrated.

Meera Sandhu

Meera Sandhu (full name: Meerindar Kaur Sandhu)

Call me old fashioned, complicated or communicationally encumbered, but I have a landline *and* a cell phone and they both take voice messages. I was putting my key into the door and I could hear the landline ringing. If I hurried, maybe I would get there in time to answer, but maybe not. And if it were important, they would call back or leave a message. I let it ring.

Although I am not completely OCD, I do indeed deploy regular routines and compulsions, some of which I am attempting to modify, and there are others in place forever. For example, it does not matter whether I am coming off a graveyard, days, or a swing shift; the first thing I always do is make myself a good meal. I refuse to listen to voicemails, or read emails until I have recharged my central nervous system, stomach, and changed into comfy clothes.

It had been a particularly difficult shift. I've been working as a cop for four years, trying to make it to the big monumental fifth year benchmark, but I still had my doubts about this career choice. The job was not getting any easier. However, after I had earned a bachelor's degree in sociology, I had to choose a direction. What can you do with a BA in sociology? I thought about taking more sociology and getting an MA, but what can you do with that degree? The other option would then be to move on to a Piled higher and Deeper (PhD), and then where would I be? One of my friends went to law school, but I knew I did not want to do three years more of student level poverty at university, either. So when my carpool mate, Nicole, went to a Vancouver Police Department recruitment lecture at the UBC Student Union Building, I tagged along to kill some time until it was carpool takeoff time. The PowerPoint presentation was not too boring, or polished, and the starting pay scale was attractive. It also turned out that after all the trouble they had in the Richmond fire department the VPD were proactively recruiting brown skinned women. And that was my ticket into the organization.

I was cutting up veggies, sautéing onions and garlic, simmering a pungent aromatic tikka masala when the landline telephone rang again. I glanced at the call display, but no name displayed and the number was not familiar so I did not pick up. Let them leave a message.

"Hi Meera, it is Morgan Elliott calling, not sure if you remember me or not. We have met a few times over the past couple of years. Well, twice actually, once at Jimmy Swanson's birthday party, and then again at the memorial service. His sister, Delia, gave me your number. Well, actually, she gave me this number, your cell phone number, and two email addresses, too. Delia is the epitome of encouragement. At any rate, this is just a social call, nothing serious, of course, I called earlier, but did not leave a message. I thought it would be better form to call back and leave a message this time. But, hey, no big deal or anything, I was just calling to see how you are doing and whether you might like to go for a coffee or something sometime. I know you work shifts and all so I'll call again sometime and see if you are available. Anyhow, I have rambled on too long, so I will say goodbye and call again tomorrow or the next day. Oh, of course, you could call me too if you wanted. Anyhow, see you later. Bye."

After dinner I listened to Morgan's message. It made me smile. So good old Delia gave Morgan my telephone number, eh, well, fine by me, I trust her screening skills. Of course, I remembered Morgan. I knew that Gayle Thibault had dumped him for some flashy French guy. I was not sure I wanted to go out with someone on the rebound, much less going out with anyone at all. My last relationship more or less ended when Carl got transferred to New York City. Careers and distances put the relationship on hiatus. Maybe we were going that direction anyway, but Carl's transfer sort of sealed the deal, and we parted.

Carl's career with the airline was taking off; get it? I guess mine was rolling along, but I was not as sure or confident of my career choice as Carl. He was so gung ho and ready to roll along the career path to success. Of course, the whole success thing was pretty elusive to get a net over. You know, who is successful and what does it mean anyways?

Evidently, my great grandfather, who I never met, was the police chief of their village in the Punjab. Maybe there was some latent genetic predisposition that pushed me to this career choice, who knows. Previously, I had always thought that sons and daughters of doctors became doctors because their parents had the pull and money to get them into medical school. I thought the same thing about lawyers, too.

Sociologically, I now know differently. Once I became a cop, I learned there were lots of cops who had a brother, father, uncle, and grandfather as cops. It was the same thing with the fire department, women notwithstanding, and family traditions of boys following a similar career path as a parent. Money had nothing to do with securing a spot. It was motivation or some other factors moving the choice. It seemed that the kids watched their parents going to work and their job satisfaction or something like that and it made them think it was a good career choice. If you thought your mother's work, as a doctor was important and worthwhile, chances are you might model her choice. If you thought her work, as a lawyer was a good thing you might want to do the same thing. Of course money mattered with university costs, but not with cops or firefighters, because money was not involved, and connections were minimized.

Whether it was fortuitous, or simply serendipitous, I just sort of stumbled into the Vancouver Police Department. This constabulary is only one hundred years old, but it sure has traditions, superstitions, cliques, and pecking order hierarchy. At first I was completely doubtful that I would fit in and survive. The first year was the worst. When you are a rookie, the hazing and learning curve are formidable. The sophomore year was a little better, but not much. The third year rolled into the fourth and even though there were times when I thought I might settle into this career, there were also many, many times when I doubted the fifth year benchmark would still find me working for the VPD.

Surviving, networking, and navigating the organization's system was something my first partner, Karen Danelchuk, knew all too well. She was my first mentor, and at times, tormentor, in the organization. Karen was also a major player in the Gay and Lesbian Police Guild. She was always tough on me, but it was for my own good, so to speak. I needed to learn street skills and organizational survival skills. "Mistakes will take you down," Karen would shout at me. And I did make mistakes.

Karen was promoted to detective sergeant. She was so happy to get out of the uniform and into plain clothes. She called the uniform a blue bag, and it made her butt look bigger than it really was. As a plain-clothes detective there were some wardrobe restrictions, but she could live with them. Of the VPD's 1214 officers in 2008, only about twenty percent are women, and from that group twelve women wore sergeant's stripes. Karen explained that the history has improved. You know, "You've come a long way, baby."

Thirty years ago, law enforcement employment discrimination against women was *blatant*. In order to work as a Royal Canadian Mounted Police Officer the candidate *must* be over five feet ten inches and weigh more than one hundred sixty pounds. Of course, this meant men only would be eligible for employment. No metric those days.

The Mounties were the first to drop this stupid discriminatory barrier for employment. History has shown that it was a dumb requirement. Moreover, research has shown that the efficacy of smaller women is much more efficient in police work that does not require brute force. If there is a fight in the pub, send in two big policemen and it is like throwing gasoline on a fire. Women officers can break up fights without getting into a fight. Maybe, it is the old adage where a man must not strike a woman. Two big Bull Moose cops can cause more problems than they can solve. They piss people off. Women can placate and solve police problems.

Karen's promotion party was a wild affair. I normally abstain from any kind of alcohol, but someone screwed up the signs on the punchbowls and I ended up drinking the "spiked" punch. That was when I met Constable Brian. The booze bent my judgment skills. Brian was straight, and a good dancer. I was reluctant to cut a rug with him, but he would not take no for an answer, and I ended up doing some version of the jive in the middle of the dance floor. Brian had trouble taking no for an answer. I learned about his reluctance to accept the notion of no, too soon.

Brian was persuasive. We went out for coffee a couple of times after respective shifts. He wanted to accelerate "the relationship" to another level. I was really reluctant relationship wise, and then I found out that he was *married*. Brian had an answer for everything. He explained that he was in the process of separating from his wife and it should have no bearing on "our relationship." I patiently explained that we did not, and would not have a relationship.

It seemed like my mistakes were mounting, both on and off the job. Karen pounded on my door and really gave it to me when she found out about Brian. "Married men are mistakes; going out with another cop like him is a mistake, too!" Karen could not keep quiet about her displeasure with my behaviour.

"I know, I know, I know," I said to Karen. "I never did anything with Brian anyway," I pleaded.

"You let him drive you home from my party. You went out for coffee with him. Are you completely nuts? He is bad news, Meera," Karen exclaimed. "He is a womanizer of the worst kind."

I started to cry. "He drove me home because I was too drunk to drive. I went out for coffee with him because I appreciated him driving me home. I didn't think it would become a big deal. I didn't think I was leading him on, or inviting anything."

"Yes, that is right, you did not *think*," Karen continued to lambaste me. "You have to learn; do not try to be so nice. It will take you down. You have got to learn. You will not make it by being nice."

After Karen's promotion I got a new partner, Ted Mah. He had close to twenty-nine years in with the department and was looking forward to retirement. He was disengaging, on the downhill slope of his career. He wanted things to go smoothly. The first time we met Ted made it clear as to what kind of a partner he wanted, "I do not want any trouble; I do not want any unnecessary problems, drama, or difficulties. No hot shots, hot dogs, rabble-rousers, career climbers, or superstars, will be welcomed as my partner. Sandhu, can you cope with that?" he asked.

"Yes, Ted," I replied, "I can cope with that."

"Good," he nodded his head, "I hate prima donnas. This place already has way too many prima donnas, and not enough team players. Everyone wants to shine at the department's expense."

We shook hands. Although Ted's agreement was unilateral, and we did not discuss *my* expectations of the partnership, I was feeling confident and happy with my new partner. The first few shifts were smooth, routine, nothing remarkable, and we were close to a well-deserved day off, when I found the baby.

We had been called to a disturbance just off Fraser Street. When we got to the address there was nothing going on, everything was quiet. We walked around the place. I went into the alley. I heard a rustling noise and an unusual sound coming from a box by the garbage can. There was a *baby* inside the box!

At first I thought the baby was dead. I screamed for Ted.

"This baby is still breathing," Ted said. "Call it in; we are going to Children's Hospital." Handing me the baby, "I'll drive."

When you turn the siren on, people know you are coming, and they are supposed to get out of the way. Some do, and some don't. Ted drove like a madman. It was fine by me. Ted's experience and driving skills are certainly superior to mine.

The Children's Hospital staff were waiting for us curbside. I handed the baby over and that was that. They would take over and everything that could be done would be done to help him. The doctor told me he was confident that we got there in time and the little guy would survive.

A couple of detectives had arrived and were beginning the investigation. Ted was explaining how we were called to the scene, and what we found when we got there. They had a couple of questions for me, and then we were back in the squad car on another call. Fortunately, the next call was just a mischief report. Some teenagers were making too much noise with their skateboards and boom boxes. An elderly man got into a shouting match with the kids and they threw a rock through his window.

"These things start out small," Ted explained, "and it is important we respond, put this small fire out before things escalate, get out of hand, and someone gets hurt. These aren't bad kids or anything, and the old guy is just old and cranky, but I have seen too many overreactions not to know what happens if we don't squash the skirmish. In the old days, nobody brought out guns to settle things. These days you never know who will pull out a gun and start firing over the smallest infraction."

I knew what Ted was talking about, and I wondered, where these guns come from anyway. I knew the old man got the rifle from a big box store, but where are kids getting these handguns?

Television makes police work look glamorous and exciting. "Sandhu, once you learn that life is not a Pepsi commercial, you will be a lot better off," Ted said with a smile.

Pepsi people have nice big white smiles, I thought to myself, not wanting to interrupt Ted's teachable moment. This is not Disneyland. Do you remember Fantasy Gardens?

"We perform a wide range of public services," Ted continued. "For poor people, cops are often serving as a social worker, psychologist, lawyer, accountant or veterinarian. These people cannot hire their own professionals. They don't have the money, and they do not know what to do anyway, even if they did have money."

"And the rich people, Ted. What about them?" I asked. "How do they see us?"

"Oh man, rich people, let me tell you about rich people," Ted began to natter. I was listening, but I was also thinking of that little baby I found in the alley. I wondered how he was doing. I wondered about his mother, how was she doing. What was her story? Who was she; where was she? Why did she leave him in the alley?

It was finally time to take a coffee break. As we were pulling into the parking lot at the Swiss Chalet restaurant, Ted was still speaking. "Rich people really see us as public servants. We work for them in a public service capacity. It is their law, and we enforce it." I saw Brian and his partner Alex were arriving at the same time through another entrance.

We parked the squad cars. Brian trotted over to say hello. I introduced him to Ted. "I am so happy for you, to meet me," Brian said with a Pepsi smile. Evidently, Ted and Alex were old friends and they were happy to chat it up.

Brian put his arm around my shoulder and said, "We heard about that baby you two found. That must have been tough. It goes to show, you never know what is going to happen next on this job, eh."

"Yes, that is right, Brian," I said calmly, politely, but firmly, while taking his arm off me. His touch gave me the creeps. The four of us sat in a booth together. Although it was not completely torturous, I would have rather not sat and chit chatted with Brian and Alex. However, I had to keep up a good appearance for my partner Ted's sake.

It seemed as though our break went on forever, and then Ted took an eternity to disengage from his prattle with Alex. Meanwhile, I endured Brian's latent and blatant moves on me. When we were finally back into our squad car, Ted turned to me and said, "Alex tells me you are having an affair with Brian."

I gasped and said, "Ted, that is so far from the truth it is pathetically funny. I am *not* having an affair with Brian Messier! I have not and will not get involved with a married man like Brian, let alone another cop. He drove me home from a party, and I had coffee with him twice after work. That is it, nothing happened. We are *not* having an affair!"

Reeling back in his seat, Ted raised his hands in a defensive gesture, "Okay, okay, I wonder why Alex would say such a thing?"

"He said it because that is what Brian told him, but that does not make it *true*," I said with an exasperated sigh.

Before we could continue, Ted had called in a 10 - 8, which translates to the dispatchers that we were back in service. Ted was an old school cop. He still used the Ten Code system all the time. 10 - 4 signals message received. 10 - 12 indicates visitors are present.

The police radio channels Ten Code system was originally developed more than seventy years ago in late 1937 by dispatcher Charlie Hooper. Ways back then, codes were preferred to words in a radio transmission for clarity and to limit the number of words in a transmission. There never was a cryptic intention. It was just the technology of the day.

In the late summer of 2005 when Hurricane Katrina hit New Orleans, federal relief was way too slow to respond, and then when they responded there was even more chaos throughout the systems. The Ten Code radio transmissions had long outlived their usefulness. When did you quit using party lines and rotary telephones? Although modern law enforcement has made some technological advances, some procedures live on and on.

Katrina showed that standardization of the ten codes, or any codes, was needed. FEMA found that there was so much variation between the agencies that confusion often followed radio and cellular telephone transmissions. This problem was easily solved. Use words not codes when communicating. Everyone can understand most of your words. Not everyone understands or translates codes.

"Ted, lay off the Ten Codes, eh." Old school dispatchers were still okay with ten codes, but younger dispatchers and by-the-book folks were less inclined to tolerate Ted's continued use of the coded system. And with that the dispatcher sent us to a serious accident at Cambie and King Edward.

When we arrived at the scene there were already four other squad cars, a giant fire fighter ladder truck, and two ambulances attending. Evidently a fatality was likely and the area had to be cordoned off and sealed so the investigators could gather evidence. Ted and I were needed to detour and help control traffic, until the traffic division arrived to take over.

People hate being detoured. Although I cannot read lips proficiently, I could translate civilian consternations and facial gestures as I directed them to detour where they had not planned on turning. People do not like to be delayed or have their travel route interrupted. I understand road rage. Everyone is in his or her vehicle going somewhere, and that is all they care about. They are inoculated from other travellers. They do not care about anything other than getting to their destination. They get mad when their route is interrupted, blocked, impeded, or detoured. And, of course, there are always those people who think they should be able to proceed through just the same. They are the exception and cannot be detoured. They want to engage in a discussion. Mind you, maybe if they knew there was a fatality they might be more tolerant and show some more patience. But, probably not, people just want to get to their destination.

It is strange how the accident carnage turns necks. It is magnetic for rubber neckers. I learned to leave the vision alone, and just do my job. Of course, it is completely different when you are a first responder. You have to get involved and get the job done. The sight always stays with me too long as a first responder. Although I am not part of the traffic cop division, we are on patrol; we still get called out to these things way too often.

It took quite a while to get everything cleared up and we went into overtime. This was a long shift. On our way back to the station Ted took a detour towards the hospital.

"Hey, Sandhu, what say we check on that little baby?" Ted asked. "I wonder how he has fared these past few hours. I am sure they got some nutrients in him."

Nodding with a smile, I said, "Yeah, he sure looked little to me. But, hey, I don't know much about babies, Ted."

"Your time will come," Ted said smiling as though he could predict my future.

Although I have not ever experienced much of a maternal drive, it was almost overwhelming while I held the little guy in the hospital. Thinking to my self and whispering quietly, I asked him, "Who are you, what is your story, and where is your mom. Do you have a family somewhere?"

Ted came strolling down the hall. Downstairs he had purchased a little plush stuffed toy dog for baby John Doe. Ted put the baby back into the basinet and softly said, "Hey little Johnny, here is a guard dog to keep an eye on you while Constable Sandhu gets some shuteye tonight. You take care little guy. Everything is going to turn out just fine."

Fatigue wise, Ted was right, I was so tired. It had been a long shift and I was glad to sign out and leave the station behind. The drive home was a good way to disengage from the day. In my mind I sorted and filed away the day's endeavours. As I approached my place I thought I saw Brian's Audi sports car pulling away.

"Nope, no way, that could not be; he would not come to where I live. I don't think," I said out loud. I knew Brian was audacious, but not to the point of crossing the line and showing up at my home. I had made things between us crystal clear. He knows exactly where I stand. I gave my head a shake and realized that I was either delusional or hallucinating because of my fatigue.

Once inside I had a snack and went straight to bed. My head hit the pillow and I fell sound asleep. I dreamed about the little baby boy we had found in the alley. I dreamed about the old man with the rifle and his altercation with the skateboarders. Then I even started dreaming about *Brian*. It was so weird. I could smell his cologne. I remembered how earlier today at the coffee shop his arm around me gave me the creeps. I felt the same way again.

Suddenly, I woke up. It was not a dream at all. A naked Brian was lying beside me. He had his arm around me and was trying to kiss me. I screamed as loud as I could, and I tried to get away from him. I was fully a wake now and flailing my arms. "What are you doing? Let me go. How did you get in here," I asked.

"Hush, hush," Brian said calmly. "I came in through the window." He held me tighter and kept trying to kiss me.

I tried to break away from his grasp, but he was just too strong. I was overpowered. "Stop it, Brian, let me go. Let me go," I yelled.

He put his hand over my mouth to try and silence my screams. "Hush, hush, Meera, you know you want me." With his other hand he tried to move my legs apart.

I was able to bite his hand and scream. "Fuck off, Brian, get out of here!"

Then he punched me in the face. "So you want it rough, eh," Brian snarled, trying to climb on top of me and pin my shoulders.

I fought back, wiggling and wriggling, but he was heavy and strong. I know there are some people who say that if a woman fights back she risks sending her attacker over the edge and ultimately getting killed. Their thinking is that it is better to get raped and live. Of course, that is thinking that he thinks and cares about consequences. He is a bastard and does not think about anything but himself. In my community, Indo women are always getting beaten up, raped, and murdered. He would not take me easily. I was able to knee him in the balls, but it was not a direct hit. And now he was definitely over the edge. He slapped my face spitting, "You bitch; now you are going to get it!"

With everything I could muster, adrenalin, and fear, I pushed him off me and slid out from under him. I started to escape out the bedroom door, but I did not get far. He grabbed my ankle, turned me around, and flipped it out from under me. I fell backwards, headfirst into the hallway floor. My head hit the floor hard.

I do not know how long I was unconscious. When I woke I was in a bed at Vancouver General Hospital. The clock on the wall was at three o'clock. Of course, I had no idea whether it was afternoon or morning. On my right side were machines and monitors. On my left side, Ted Mah and Karen Danelchuk were sprawled in two chairs, side by side. They were both sound asleep.

Although it was quite painful, I was able to smile at the sight of Ted and Karen. Now I looked forward to reporting to everyone that I knew as a true fact that Karen had slept with Ted. I thought it was funny. Of course, my old boyfriend Carl used to remind me that some of the things I found bone-slapping funny were not all that funny to others. The fact that Ted and Karen were sound asleep in the hospital room allowed me to create the joke of them sleeping together. I thought it was funny. I know I could find some others who thought it was funny. Maybe Karen and Ted would think it was stupid, but I thought it was funny. What a sight to see, the two of them sound asleep, side by side.

"Hey, lovebirds," I croaked out softly.

Ted, dead to the world, heard nothing, but Karen stirred, and looked up at me. "Hi, how are you feeling?" she said.

"Just great," I moaned. "Where am I?"

Karen scoffed, "This is VGH. Meera, do you know who did this to you?"

"Brian Messier," I winced with pain. "Get him Karen!"

And with that, well before breakfast was served, Karen had arrested Brian, placed him behind bars and was waiting for bail court. He was surprised with the speed of the arrest that fell upon him. He hardly had time to put much of a story together. Of course, it did not take Brian long to plead not guilty and concoct a lie ridden account of his side of the story.

The detectives told Brian they had overwhelming evidence against him. Karen said that at first he appeared like a deer in headlights. He reluctantly agreed that he had indeed been to my place, but he claimed that I had invited him earlier in afternoon while in the parking lot of the coffee shop. "Just check with my partner, Alex Buchanan. He will tell you that at the end of our shift he asked what my plans were for the evening. I told him I had a date with Meera Sandhu scheduled. Check it out," Brian challenged the detectives.

Brian claimed the sex was consensual. When Karen confronted him with my injuries, Brian claimed to not know anything about them. He said it was rough sex, but he knew nothing of any injuries. "Ms. Sandhu was asleep when I left her house. She was not injured in any way shape or form. When I left she had a big smile on her face."

Karen was incensed with Brian's contention that someone else must have broken in after he had left. Someone else did it, not him. "You expect me to believe that, Brian?" Karen said with distain. "We have enough evidence to put you away for a long, long time. So Brian good luck with that version of the story, do you actually think a jury will buy your hogwash? Not a chance," Karen spit while she spoke.

Brian smiled back at her saying, "This will never get that far. I will be out of here before you can do the lesbo wild thing. You have nothing on me. I will never see a jury!"

And so the criminal justice process began with me as a participant in a role that I would rather not serve. I attended the arraignment. Brian looked at me and winked. Then there was the preliminary trail. The evidence was adequate and we proceeded to the trial. Brian was suspended from the VPD until the trial was over, under the auspices of innocent until proven guilty. To my amazement, Brian was adamant and continued to claim he was not guilty. "It was not Brian Messier who committed this crime," his lawyer told the jury. "When Mr. Messier left Ms. Sandhu's home, she was safe, sound, and smiling."

Brian sat in the prisoner's box looking smug, and confident he could beat the charge. Karen was disgusted, and when she found out that the Senior Crown Prosecutor, Joseph Tweedsmuir, had offered Brian the opportunity to plead guilty to a lesser charge and avoid the trial, she went wild with anger saying, "That idiot thinks he can roll the dice and beat this charge. He is rolling snake eyes!"

Karen was not too kind towards Senior Crown Prosecutor, Mr. Tweedsmuir. But she understood his job, as the crown's representative was to try and avoid lengthy and costly trials. And this one proved as lengthy and costly as any other of the trials that travel through the criminal justice system's process. It just seemed to go on and on with one legal wrinkle followed by another application appeal. A costly trial does not just involve the pecuniary aspects of money and financial costs associated with fees and disbursements; it is also the costs and tolls taken on your mental health, physical health, and social standing. As a victim, I hated the way the world looked at me, the way they treated me, and all the things that being a victim involves.

Brian was convicted. The jury deliberated briefly and came back with a guilty verdict. Brian appealed, and for a brief time it appeared that he might get a new trial based on a legal technicality. A new trial meant we would go through it all over again. "Fine with me," I said, "I am in for the long run. However long this takes is just however long it takes. I am good to go to the end."

Justice, fairness, due process, and the legal system were all abstract concepts until the night Brian Messier broke into my home, beat me to a pulp, and raped me multiple times. I look at those concepts differently now. They are concrete concepts now. I look at life differently now. Life is different now.

Next month I am going to get married to Morgan Elliott. He is a lovely, decent, upstanding man, and we are going to be married. At first my parents were not too happy with me marrying a white man (actually his colour is a bit on the pinkish ruddy red side). They had always held hope I would settle with a nice suitor from India. It never happened and they dealt with it.

Delia Swanson, my maid of honour, secured a beautiful venue for the ceremony. We were going to be married at the Shaughnessy United Church at Thirty Third and Granville.

The wedding plans and details would be overwhelming, but my entourage of friends and colleagues has pulled together. I am excited. It is a new beginning to a new life. And even though everyone else tried to discourage our application, we recently file adoption papers to try and adopt baby John Doe. I never lost track of him. I visited as often as I could. He has been in foster care all this time. Morgan and I want to try and give him a home with us. Of course, the paperwork, files, and applications are taking forever. These things take time. We have started the process.

Last month marked my fifth year as a Constable with the VPD.

The Fifth Wheel

WIKIPEDIA WRITES:

a cousin is a relative with whom a person shares one or more ancestors (other than a parent, child, ancestor, descendant, sibling, descendant/child of sibling, or sibling of an ancestor/parent). However in common parlance, "cousin" normally means "first cousin"

Systems of "degrees" and "removals" are used in the English-speaking world to describe the exact relationship between two cousins (in the broad sense) and the ancestor they have in common...

‡

Jimmy Swanson and his dozens of cousins were a powerful force with which to contend.

One time I tried to explain to Jimmy that I felt like a "fifth wheel" with his group. He heard me, but did not listen.

Indeed he went on to explain the history of fifth wheel coupling and horse drawn carriages. Jim could re-frame anything and everything. He made lemonade out of lemons. Clients loved him. They would seemingly have an insurmountable problem and Jimmy reframed it into a positive production.

Angry clients were the best. They would have some big beef and would rant to Jimmy about the issues. He would listen, talk it over, and actually give them nothing. But, the client felt they got something and felt better. Jimmy said clients who were encouraged did much better than those who were discouraged.

It took me too long to finally understand how it all works. Originally I thought it was because they were west side and I was east side that made the difference.

Jimmy took no sides. It was all the same to him.

For me, the penny dropped when we were at a big accountant's conference. Jim and I were standing off to the side working on hockey pool calculations when two important people approached us.

Quickly sticking out his hand to shake Jimmy said, "Hello Mr. Important Person, have you met my cousin Michael Lee?"

We both shook our heads. No, we have not met. I come from a background where the "truth" is paramount. I wanted to tell them that I was not really Jimmy's cousin and I do not know why he says these things.

My girlfriend, Amy, explained how it works. True, Gerald Westonmeyer and Jimmy are first cousins. But, much like in the Indo-Canadian culture where every adult woman is addressed as "auntie" (even when they are not your real auntie), Jimmy refers to all his good friends as his cousins. Albeit distant cousins as it were.

When Jimmy died I was ever so honoured that he often would refer to me as a cousin.

I miss him. I miss him every day, in so many ways, I cannot begin to say.

R.I.P. cousin, I hope we meet again some day.

Metaphoric Mountains

In the fall of 1975 I was hired as a Stack Attendant at the University of British Columbia's Main Library. Next to working as a lifeguard, or ski lift operator in Banff, Stack Attendant was one of the best jobs I had ever held. Earlier that spring I had completed all of the course requirements for a Bachelor of Arts degree with a major in History and a minor in Political Science. What should I do post graduation? I had options, but I was not clear which direction to take next. I needed a job. Of course, I could try and find another waitress job or one as a retail clerk, and then I saw the UBC Main Library was hiring. A stern looking administrator, Erik de Byron, interviewed me. Two days later, I was hired. Three days after that, I started.

My first day was a warm September morning; I arrived to work early, sat on the edge of the water fountain out front and waited for the library to open its doors. I did not know employees entered through a back door that opened at six. The library was a grand looking building. It had been built fifty years earlier in 1925 at the completion of the Scopes trial in Tennessee.

Basil Stuart Stubbs, the Head Librarian, did orientation tours for new employees. The tour started with our small group of six standing outside the building. You could tell, Basil loved the place, "Anything, you want to know about anything," he said, "we will have it inside this library. And, if by some chance we do not have the specific title the patron is searching, we will get it through Interlibrary Loans."

Delores, the tall blonde standing next to me muttered, "Yeah, yeah," under her breath. She was getting bored at a similar rate to my getting curious and excited about the place.

Stubbs pointed to the Library's entrance, "See those two sculptures?" he invited our line of sight.

"Sir, aren't those gargoyles," Delores asked interrupting Stubbs' speech, "and not really sculptures per se?"

Stubbs stopped, glanced over our direction, "Sorry, you are?" he asked.

"Delores, RBC," she replied. RBC stood for Reserve Book Collection.

"Actually, they are indeed sculptures," he explained. "Architecturally, a gargoyle, although appearing similar to sculpture, is an old French word meaning throat. A gargoyle usually is a part of a gutter system where water is directed and terminated from the mouth as a spout. These are not gargoyles, they are Al Fresco sculptures."

Delores nodded a deferential understanding as Stubbs continued to explain how the sculpture on the left showed a monkey holding a scroll that says EVOLUT. The sculpture on the right is a weird looking bearded man holding a scroll that reads FUNDA. These sculptures were appropriate decorations above the library's entrance. It seemed funny to think that fifty years earlier when this building was completed the Scopes trail had just ended. Social context and architecture collide with a monkey above the library's door.

John Scopes was a teacher convicted of teaching evolution in Dayton, Tennessee. It became known as the Monkey Trial. The defence team included Clarence Darrow, while the prosecution team boasted William Jennings Bryan. These legal giants from the mid nineteen twenties argued the facts of the case. The jury found Scopes guilty of teaching Darwinist theories of evolution to Dayton High

School students and he received a fine. Scopes had violated Tennessee law. The textbook was illegal and banned from use in schools.

Those sculptures above the entrance to the library represented education and learning pedagogy from the era when the library building was constructed. Little did I know eighty years after the Scopes trial that my daughter, Colleen, would work on the legal team defending James Chamberlain, a British Columbia teacher who attempted to use banned books in the classroom. The local suburban Surrey school board stated books that presented same-sex parents violated the community's values and they were banned from being used in classrooms.

After way too many protracted legal arguments, testimonies, briefs, and legal battles, late in 2002 the Supreme Court of Canada overturned the British Columbia's Court of Appeal decision to ban books showing same-sex relationships. The Chief Judge of Canada's top court, Justice Beverly McLachlin, ruled that a school board could not impose their religious values and ban the books. It was now legal to teach pupils about family diversity.

Colleen was crazy angry about how much money the Surrey School District zealots spent on legal fees. "They spent millions of taxpayer's dollars to pursue religious ideology," she would say, coming close to a scream. "Mom, do you know how many teachers they could have hired to teach kids how to READ?"

I understood, and I admired her sense of justice and passion. Whether it was the Scopes trial or banned books like *One Dad, Two Dads, Brown Dads, Blue Dads,* people pushing religious intolerance had to be dealt down. They simply cannot continue with an agenda that is narrow and disrespectful to regular people.

Of course, history has shown the relationship between religion and politics has always had a rough ride. Although I remain benign to politics and governance, I have never understood the anthropological or social psychological ramifications of religion. I know anthropologists report every culture they have ever come across has some sort of religion or supernatural believe system. I remember hearing about missionaries who tried to tell the pygmies that belief in the river, as a god was wrong. The missionaries showed the pygmies the "real god." The pygmies killed the missionaries.

After the death of my youngest son, Jimmy, my husband Russell became religious. It started slowly and then the next thing I knew he was just completely immersed with religious explanations and their platitudes, too. John Lennon said, "Whatever gets you through the night, it's all right." So Russ found religion. It got him through the night all right, but it only aggravated me.

My counsellor, Dr. McNicol, explained that Russell's behaviour was not completely abnormal given the context. She encouraged me to try and be a little more tolerant and accepting of Russell's religion. I tried to tolerate his new found lifestyle and belief system, but I felt like one of the pygmies. He was driving me nuts.

I went for more counselling. We went together for couples counselling. It was just no use. I could not cope. I could not cope with Jimmy's death. I could not cope with Russell's religious rantings. Dr. McNicol was great. She explained, statistically speaking, many couples experience a tremendous amount of stress with the death of a child. Neither of us blamed the other for Jimmy's death, but just the sight of Russell and the sound of his religious rants were pushing me over the edge. I had to get away from him for a while. Maybe a break and a change of scenery would help.

My lifelong friend, Margaret "Maggie" Westonmeyer, was Russell's sister. She telephoned and suggested we take a trip together to Tofino. "Karen lets do it, let's just get away. There is a spectacular spa and restaurant at Wickininish. We can lounge around, comb the beach, and have some good times," she said smiling at me. Good times were the old catch phrase we would always banter back and forth. And goodness knows we need some good times.

Jimmy's death turned everything upside down and turned it all around. It was the worst of the worst of times. Maggie's son, Gerald, had been with Jimmy on a hiking excursion on Grouse Mountain. When the boys realized they were lost with nightfall approaching fast.

Gerald decided to stay still and he waited for searchers, while Jimmy ploughed ahead trying to find his own way out. He fell to his death, but it took over two months to find his body that had been hidden in the underbrush. Meanwhile my daughter, Delia, and Gerald began an affair.

Perplexing to say the least, Maggie and I were astounded to hear about Delia and Gerald's affair. And then, on the other hand, it was not that unusual given the circumstances. Although I could not condone, I was able to understand. Nonetheless, they are cousins!

Delia, my oldest daughter, explained that it was actually a one-night stand that occurred in a moment of weakness when they had heard that Jimmy's body had been recovered. It was not a full-fledged affair, but people like to talk. It gave them something to talk about.

Nietzsche said, "If you have a why (to live), you can stand any how." Of course, he is also the same guy who said, "That which does not destroy us makes us stronger." I was not destroyed. I was not depressed, maybe repressed, but I was not suicidal or anything. I was drifting without an anchor. Postmenopausal, an empty nester, with a husband turned to religion, I needed some good times.

Maggie and I had a great time in Tofino. We stayed at the Middle Beach Lodge. Down the road the Wickininish spa was indeed spectacular. We walked up and down Long Beach. The surf, sand, and wind were so refreshing. And although Maggie's son had not died that day on Grouse Mountain, she had been though so much agony, too. She is such a good friend. The late, great, Harry Chapin, had a song with a lyric line saying, "Old friends, they mean so much more to me than a new friend can. Because they know where you are, and they know where you have been." Maggie my good "old" friend, listened, talked, and we walked. It was a good time.

Yes, and as they say, all good things must come to an end. We returned to our respective homes. It had been great to relax with Maggie. I felt energized and I was determined to try and make a go of it with Russ. We married for better or worse, sickness and health, and I owed it to him to give the marriage another try. We went for more counselling. This time we went to a new couple's counsellor that Russ had heard about. Soon I started to realize that I was the proverbial horse led to water, but unwilling to drink.

And then it came to me, after all these counselling sessions that I had started to develop a level of depth and interest in various techniques, theories, and styles. Religion seemed to work for Russ. *Nothing* was working for me. I had no complaints or criticisms about any of the counsellors we had seen. Rather, my curiosity had increased. I decided to go back to my roots and explored the PhD programme in counselling at UBC. It was a plan, a focus, a goal, a direction, and I wanted to learn what it was all about. Maybe I could make a contribution. Maybe I could make a difference.

I had been a good wife, a good homemaker, a good mother, and now I needed to be *good to me*. Actually, I got the idea from Dr. McNicol when she explained that I was no good to nobody while I was down and out. If I could pick myself up and look after my needs I could then tend to others. It made sense. Of course when I told Dr. McNicol of my plan to pursue a PhD, she was a little more guarded with her advice.

"Karen, you have got to understand the PhD journey can be a terribly gruesome endeavour, and it may take a long time to complete. On the other hand, there are some women planning a trip to the top of Mount Everest. Maybe you could do that instead, because it is similar in many ways. One gets started at the foot of the mountain. The sun is shining, birds are singing, spirits are high, and it seems like such a good idea. The challenge comes when one starts to climb above the tree line. The winds starts whirling, its gets colder, the sun sets, and one wonders whether it is worth the toll when the top is still at such a distance. Why would you want to do it?" she asked.

I had an appropriate answer. I smiled, and said, "Because it is there."

Of course, it was way easier said than done. Developing an idea was one thing, getting accepted was another. I checked out the brochures, entrance requirements, and cringed. Although on paper, I met the entrance requirements, there were still some hurdles to hop. There was this little matter of a standardized entrance exam to take. I had not taken an exam since an eternity of time had passed. I was okay though because there was a time when I was good at exams. I was cautiously confident. I knew if I could get over the exam hurdle and get to the interview I could make it in. Now that was where I took a stumble.

After I passed the entrance exam I was awarded an interview with the admissions committee. I would have arrived earlier, but I had a wardrobe malfunction. I was determined to wear my lucky jade and pearl pendant necklace. However, I had not been lucky for a while. Thus, I had not worn the necklace in a while and the thin gold chain links were tangled in a tight knot. Why hadn't I stored it better was beyond me. At first my efforts to detangle made it worse, the knot got bigger. I thought about giving up and going bare necked to the interview. Of course, no quitting allowed in my domain. But the time kept ticking, and I knew there were other issues like which jacket, route to drive, and where to park. Finally, I used a toothpick to separate the strands, and presto changeo it came undone.

The drive was fine, traffic not too bad, and I took my favourite scenic route along Northwest Marine Drive. However, parking was terrible, and has been since the eighties when the administration moved from surface parking lots to parkades. Undaunted and undeterred I arrived with a spot of time to spare. Maybe this idea was a mistake. When I looked around the room, everyone else was young and beautiful. My confidence sagged.

When the door to Seminar Room B in the Counselling Psychology Office opened, a pleasant looking professor looked around the room and called my name, "Karen Swanson."

I rose up from my waiting room chair, trotted into the seminar room for my admissions interview, and was guided towards the applicant's chair. The committee consisted of three professors, Dr. Joel Adams, the senior full professor, and chair of the admissions committee, who introduced the other two saying, "Good afternoon Mrs. Swanson."

"Oh, you can call me Karen," I interrupted.

"Yes, well, fine," Adams cleared his throat and introduced Dr. Leigh, and Dr. Devlin. "Please take a seat Mrs. Swanson."

Pleasantries aside, Adams opened a file; I could see my name up top, "Thank you for coming this afternoon Mrs. Swanson," he began, "this is a semi standardized interview where the admissions committee gathers direct information from prospective applicants. As you know we have far more applicants than we have spaces in our programme. We are constrained to ten applicants per academic year."

Interrupting his monologue, I nodded with a smile, saying, "Oh, I did not know that."

"Yes, well, fine," he continued, "This is our opportunity to interview prospective applicants. The majority of applicants all have excellent undergraduate transcripts and high scores on the entrance exam. This interview helps us try and determine suitability to our programme. Maybe we could start with you explaining your motivation for applying to our programme, and why we should consider granting a space to a middle-aged housewife."

This was not what I had expected. I actually do not know precisely what I expected, but the middle-aged slag and housewife slur were not well received. My blood pressure and temper were rising; I took a breath and began by saying, "With respect Dr. Adams, the Canadian Human Rights Code notwithstanding regarding age discrimination, I am reminded of Twain's assertion that middle-aged people are always ten years older than me. Do you think I am old? At age fifty-four I bring maturity, wisdom, and experience to your programme. My motivation is simple. If tomorrow is the first day of the rest of my life, let's get started. I would like to learn counselling psychology pedagogy, theories, techniques, and applications. I feel that I can make a contribution to the field. This is not a new hobby. I am certainly committed and motivated, neither of which are likely measured in an applicant's interview such as this. Thank you for your time." I got up and briskly walked out.

I did not start crying until I was safely inside the car. I drove home with the wipers on both inside and outside. What I fool I was, and who was I trying to fool anyway? It was true, I *am* a middle-aged housewife, and I made a fool of myself.

I have climbed the hill and now I am sliding down the other side to an older age. It just happened too fast. One day I was a little girl looking at the calendar waiting with six months to go until my birthday would arrive, "Oh, I will never make it until then. It is too far to go. I need my birthday present wish now," I would lamely explain to my mother. Nowadays, all I need to do is blink, and another birthday appears.

When I got home, the house was quiet, nobody home, and nothing happening. I plopped myself down in the parlour and heaved a heavy sigh. Russ telephoned and asked how my interview went. I replied with, "It was fine, basically okay, but they only have a few spaces so I do not have my hopes up."

"Hey, whats for dinner," Russ asked. My adrenalin was rising, and with thoughts of booking an appointment for anger management counselling, when he continued, "I got a reservation at Bishops. If you have not got anything planned already, let's go out."

"Sure, Russ, Bishops sounds great."

"Delia and Colleen say they can come, too."

"Yes, great, thanks Russ, a family dinner out will be nice."

One week later I received a letter of acceptance into the UBC Counselling Psychology programme. I was so surprised. It was a form letter that had some individualization, but it had the magic words, "Welcome to the PhD programme."

I telephoned Maggie with my good news. She was ecstatic, "Oh Karen, I knew you could do it!"

"Well I haven't done anything, yet," I explained. "Getting in is one thing, graduating and getting out is another."

Maggs raised her voice to a higher decibel level saying, "You go girl, it is just one step at a time! You go girl!" I held the receiver a couple of inches from my ear and smiled.

And so it began, proceeding under the auspices of tomorrow standing as the first day of the rest of my life, I was going to get started. I never expected that it would be easy. I knew it presented challenges and more hurdles to hop. But, Maggs was correct; it was one hurdle at a time. I thought about the tortoise and hare proverb. Or maybe the race did not necessarily go to the swiftest, but to those that kept running. "Pace the race," she would say.

"Dual relationships are prohibited under the psychology code of conduct and ethical behaviours," Dr. McNicol explained. "I cannot be your counsellor and colleague at the same time," she explained. "It would be a boundary conflict."

I was pleased. No, actually, I was honoured to think she now thought of us as "colleagues." I understood the dual relationships edict. Boundaries between clients and counsellors are important. The boundaries help and protect all involved. Besides, I did not need any more personal counselling, I needed education. Colleagues, new friends and fellow travellers were important. This was especially the case as I began to tackle the catalogue of required and elective courses.

First year of the PhD programme there was no institutional departmental coercion to pick an area of specialization. The doctoral seminar was a required course where I met the other nine members of my cohort. The purpose of the seminar was to facilitate orientation and get us going down the correct path. It is not too easy to stray off track. Although the original marathon metaphor that Dr. McNicol had described made sense, now I had the baseball analogy batted by seminar leader Dr. Sanford Corigliano.

"Step one; get accepted into the programme, which is much like leaving the dugout's on deck zone and approaching the batter's box at home plate. Not just anyone gets to approach the plate. Then, you must take all the required and elective courses, which will get you to the first base. Now you are really in the game. You did not strike out, pop out, or ground out. Next, after collecting all the practicum, intern, and external clinical counselling hours you move to second base. Halfway to home, standing on second you will glance over to third base. You get there after completing and successfully passing the doctoral comprehensive and candidate qualifying examinations. And there you are, standing on third base, you can see your family and friends sitting in the stands waving, encouraging you home. All you have left is the grand slam royal research original field contribution dissertation to do and then you will slide across home plate. That is it," Corigliano said with a smirkish smurfish smile, "Go get fitted for a cap and grad gown."

"Yes, no problem, the baseball scenario certainly sounds way easier than the marathon analogy," I said to the student sitting beside me. We looked at each other and shook our heads with a slight nod. The cohort consisted of nine other students. We were a mixed bunch. Sure, some of those twenty-something gorgeous girls I saw primping in the counselling psych student lounge were there, but they all had their stories, too.

Michael Graham was one of the first fellow students I met in the cohort. Previously, he had been working as a ski instructor at Whistler in the winters, and a fishing guide at Painter's Lodge near Vancouver Island's Campbell River in the summers. Although at age thirty-four, Mike is twenty years my junior, he was wise beyond his years. We went for coffee to debrief and confabulate on the programme's process and procedures. We quickly became good friends, compatriots, and compadres, too. I knew Michael was way more intelligent than me. I knew that because he could process information quickly, and reframe it into an understandable ditty.

"These statistical equations are just ridiculous," I would say with frustration. "It is ludicrous to think those correlation coefficients can make sense to anyone."

But, it made sense to Mike. I tried to get it. I really did try. Prior to going to class, I had read the book, reviewed the research, put on my helmet and shield, and paid attention to the lecture. I understood the value of quantitative statistical explanations of social constructs. "If you cannot count it, how do you know it is there?"

After class Mike and I would go to the UBC Barn Café to debrief. Sometimes Stephanie Meyers would join us, but she often had to go to work at her waitress job. "So, okay, I get the part about not squaring the correlation coefficient when the standard error is greater than the confidence interval, but the blau, blau, blee is just beyond me," I would say with frustration over not being able to "get it" the first or second time around.

Michael would smile, patiently pull out a pencil, and say, "No Karen, you are looking at it from the wrong angle. It is blee, blee, blee and then blaw, blau."

"Whoa, whoa, whoa, yes, I get it," I would say with a good level of glee. The loonie has dropped, and the light was turned on bright, "I can see it so clearly now." Once Mike had reframed the concept into a more understandable frame of reference I was able to use it and build on top of it. He was so smart. He could understand things so quickly, put the pieces together, and then take them apart explaining them to Stephanie and me.

Mike was great. Next day I saw Prof. Bruno Zamburn waiting for the elevator. He nodded hello and I replied with, "Hubert Blalock from UW was on to something with spurious path analyses, eh?" Zamburn smiled, nodded, and simply said, "yes." He knew: I got it.

I cried and cried forever and a day when Michael told me he was quitting, dropping out of the programme. He had lost his momentum and motivation to carry on with all the nonsense involved in this journey. Now, he was not a complete fool, he filed leave of absence papers just in case he wanted to come back in a year. "C'mon Karen, be happy for me," he said as I sniffled and gave him a bone crushing hug goodbye. "I'll stay in touch. You are okay, you can fly, you don't need me," he said smiling with his hands holding my shoulders firmly.

"Sure, sure, I know, but I will miss your handsome face, and stupid sense of humour," I explained.

Michael moved on. He met an attractive, erudite woman who ran a bed and breakfast inn on Vancouver Island. He was happy. He had a purpose. I took Russ over to the island and we had dinner with Michael and Elizabeth. We stayed the night and took the early morning ferry home the next day. It was okay, but I still felt weird knowing that Michael was so much smarter than me, but had given it up, and I was still plodding along the PhD path. "What's wrong with this picture," I wondered.

"Pardon?" Russ asked.

I tried explaining my thoughts to Russ, but then he started doing a religious spin and I tuned him out. I pulled out my notebook, retreating back to my work, "Sorry, Russ, I have got to get some stuff done by Monday. I am in bit of a bind."

"Sure dear," he nodded, "pitter-patter you better get at 'er."

And I did get to it. I worked my butt off, morning, noon, and night. Russ and I were still hanging together. We were at a truce. Or should I say I was at a relationship respite. I realized that it seemed easier to stay with him than to leave. So I stayed. It made him and the girls happy that we were still together. I missed Jimmy. I thought about him every day. I wished he was here to talk to and scheme together. Life goes on, so they say. It is a different life without Jimmy, but it goes on anyway. I think he would be proud of me.

I was studying all the time. They renovated the Main Library. When it was originally built in 1925 earthquakes were not on the architectural radar as in these days. The original library had six floors of books all connected by a unifying stacking structure that went from the first to sixth floor. Books are heavy; in an earthquake one floor would pancake on another. Thus, the building changed with earthquake proofing. But, the "feeling" remained, as did the sculptures of monkey and scholar.

Normative and institutional behaviours change. It is like evolution, but not the Scopes kind. We would like to think these changes are for the better, but that is not always the case. I remember back in the seventies when the fathers of the university allowed my friends to construct "share-a-ride" signs and place them at strategic spots around exit routes from the university. Back then hitchhiking was normal and institutionally endorsed. They had signs posted by zone or neighbourhood: Kitsilano, Capilano, North, Van, West Van, Marpole, Burnaby, and others. All you had to do was stand by your sign and wait for someone to drive by and pick you up. It was environmentally friendly ahead of its time. Back then we thought fuel prices were too high. However, norms change and the signs came down after the university's lawyers deemed the liability issues incurred if students were assaulted or robbed after standing at a hitchhiking signpost outweighed any benefits to the university.

Norms and frequency distributions also change in counselling psychology practices. One of the postdoc students, Ursula Derozia, was putting together a departmental colloquium on the current prevalence and incidence of eating disorders in adolescents. Stephanie and I attended. We were so surprised to hear Ursula describe her internship experience at St. Paul's Hospital Eating Disorder Clinic. Evidently, the number of adolescent boys requiring treatment for anorexia nervosa has increased exponentially in the past decade with the highest mortality rate of any psychiatric condition. Moreover, Ursula explained that their suicide rate is sixty times greater than the general population.

"Of course, their suicide rate is concomitant with other psychological conditions such as anxiety and depression." Ursula continued, commenting that, "We all know girls threaten suicide more frequently, however, adolescent boys complete suicide at a far great rate."

Someone at the back of the room asked whether adolescents' "successful suicide rates" were rising. This started a discussion on successful suicides, completed suicides, and political correctness, nomenclature and descriptions of behaviours. I was still fresh from yesterday's discussion in my cognitive assessment seminar concerning the utility of clinical terms and confusion describing clients' conditions. That is, imbecile, moron, idiot, and retard were all once good clean clinical terms used to describe cognitive functioning. No one got mad or thought any of these terms were inappropriate. Nowadays using those terms is politically incorrect and offensive. Myself, I wonder about the value of political correctness. Offensiveness, on the other hand, is never needed.

Anxiety is contagious. It is a state and trait condition. I do not have the trait, but I can slide into the state. I was cruising along clearing the programme's hurdles one at a time, doing just fine, I was not anxious or overly concerned about the internship requirement until Stephanie and Allison Maltby got me going on the issue. They were closing in on respective placements, and I had not even given too much consideration to where I would complete the internship. I had thought about becoming a psychological geriatrician because it is such a booming area with a shortage of practitioners, but after listening to Ursula's presentation I was interested in adolescent eating disorders. I was lucky enough to land a spot at Children's' Hospital.

It was a great place to work. I was a *paid* intern. At the first psychology department meeting, I met one of the other interns, Maria Reynolds. We had crossed paths before, but Maria was a year a head of me in the programme. She was working with children who were receiving cancer treatments. Her work was certainly important and sounded interesting. The psychologists in Maria's area were participating in a progressive programme in pain management. The children received traditional pain pharmacological medications as well as some psychological treatments, too.

Maria explained, "I don't care what will work, when a kid is in pain we have to help alleviate the symptoms. If traditional pharmacological meds work, then great, no problem, case closed. But, if traditional methods do not work we have to try something else. Life is too short to be in pain. Physical or mental pain must be dealt down. Our group has been exploring other approaches the range from acupuncture, hypnosis, to cognitive behavioural therapies."

Michael called cognitive behavioural therapies (CBT) the current clinical counselling crescent wrench and he thought the theory and applied techniques may have become just a bit too popular as a psychological panacea. He had a valid point and I knew where he was coming from, but the anorexic adolescents needed to think differently.

Modifications to thinking and behaviour were necessary or face mortality. When the anorexic looks in a mirror the reflection is that of a fat obese person, when in fact the opposite is true. However, they do not see it that way. Validity may be in the eye of the beholder. They think food is the enemy and begin starvation diets.

I attended a group treatment session where the patients were all put in a room together. They were seated with food in front of them. The psychologist started talking them through the eating process saying, "Okay, take a bite. Now feel the food going through your body. Think of it as fuel. If a car has no fuel it will not work. Take another bite and think of it as fuel. The food keeps you alive. The food is fuel for your body. The food allows your body to keep working. You can control the food you eat without letting the food control you."

It was interesting. Maria and I had lunch together and she explained one of the pain treatments they were using with cancer patients. She called it "Mind over Matter." The patient is guided through a process where they envision an army of white corpuscles marching en masse toward the area of pain. The army attacks the area and chips away at the pain enemy. Another way was to have the patient envision a white light like laser beaming down to the area of cancer and blasting it apart. I thought both were beholden on violent fighting warlike scenarios. And Maria confirmed: Killing cancer is a war.

I missed Michael's cynicism. He would likely take some level of umbrage with Maria and her colleagues' approach, saying it was less than scientific and maybe slightly unethical because it misleads the patients. It would give them false hopes with a modern white-coated shamanistic hype with hokum, but no evidence based validity. Mike often said, "Psychology is still a soft science, if it can be considered a science at all. The craft of counselling is more art than science. The heterogeneity of pedagogy is a perfect example. The harder sciences like physics or chemistry empirically build one theory on top of another. Psychology is scattered. There is no common language or universal practice paradigm. A Canadian chemist can converse with a Chinese chemist. They speak chemistry. Both understand and practice similar principles. Psychology is scattered."

When I mentioned this notion to Maria her response was a measured monologue stating that, "You think so called modern medicine is not a little more than slightly unethical with such a heavy reliance on so called science and empty empiricism. We could learn a lot from the shaman. Western ethnocentric science is short sighted. Aboriginal medicine men were effective, curing their people with time tried traditional methods that worked. Their place in the community's structure was solid with good standing, until the colonial conquerors told them their methods were wrong. Chinese medicine is another good example with thousands of years of effectiveness. Pills, pills, pills, and more pills cannot persuade me. Promises from pharmacological science are not the be-all end-all. Pejorative people, who dismiss mind over matter as too soft, too unscientific, are missing the point and the connection between the brain as a physiological organs and the mind's power to heal through positive thoughts."

"Yes, I know what you mean, Maria," I said trying to explain my position. "I think you are into some good stuff. You are really doing good work. Could you email me some key literature references, I would like to read more, and learn about the issues. It is not that I have any spare time, what with all the programme's hurdles I have yet to hop, but I would like to read more and learn about the possibilities of this area."

Maria was great. She was such a generous colleague. Her patience and dedication were admirable. We agreed to have lunch again next week, same time, same place. It was encouraging and I felt good about my internship. I took the bus home. Parking was such a hassle, and taking the bus allowed me to do some reading.

Russ had dinner in progress when I arrived home. He was really trying hard to be supportive and keep our marriage alive. Russ was still pushing the religious agenda, but he did dial down some of the rhetoric and I was trying to be more tolerant of his needs. Evidently, he needed religion. "Hi dear, I am home," I announced coming through the door like a million times I have done before, "Dinner smells delectable. What are you cooking?"

He came bustling out to meet me wearing his favourite apron with an upside down Nike logo and slogan "Chef Just Did It." Tea towel slung over his shoulder and big warm smile on his face, he said, "Hello darling, you are just in time to taste my bouillabaisse and seafood casserole."

"Wow, sounds great," I said planting an affectionate kiss on him, "will you give me a minute to put my stuff down and get out of these clothes."

"Oh, yes, no hurry," he replied, "the biscuits are still in the oven."

"Okay, I will get changed."

Dinner was nice. It was comfortable. Russ had evolved into a good gourmet cook. We talked about our respective days. Russ threw in some religious overtones when I explained my initial meeting and clinical interview with May Lee Chen. Today the fifteen-year-old twin was admitted back into the hospital because her parents were at their wits end with her refusal to eat. In the past two years she and her identical twin sister Lily had been in and out of the hospital three times. Each time they both recovered enough to be discharged to outpatient status. This time, however, May Lee presented with significant weight loss and deteriorating cognitive functioning abilities. May Lee was not able to pass the mental status exam.

I was assigned as part of the interdisciplinary team some supervised responsibilities for May Lee's care. The team consisted of a social worker, primary care nurse, psychiatrist, and I was the psychologist assigned to her case. First I met with her parents, and then I met with both Lily and May Lee together to try and develop a new treatment plan. Previous plans had failed, now something new needed to be implemented as May Lee was closer to death than ever before. She refused to eat and intravenous forced feeding was considered.

Although I thought I knew a little about monozygotic twins, I soon learned I knew nothing. Certainly, Lily and May Lee showed many of the typical traits like low birth weight, five weeks premature, similar mannerisms, attitudes, and personality traits, but the bottom line was Lily was currently functional, May Lee was not. Traditional thoughts and twin theories were not as helpful as Lily's simple statement, "I don't know what is wrong with May Lee? She changed or something, I don't know?"

The nature–nurture theories of personality were old and tired, but I knew nothing to replace them. Clearly, Lily and May Lee were monozygotic identical twins with as close to an identical genetic blueprint as possible. Their mannerisms and attitudes were also so similar that psychometric measures showed no differences. Their personalities, to date, were similar. Like most twins they share a bond that started in the womb and carries with them through life stages. As toddlers they were inseparable, they spoke in their own coded language. When they started school some well-meaning teachers thought that separating them would be a good idea to help develop separate identities and independence from one another. The teachers were wrong. Separation caused more problems than anticipated. Both began spiralling downwards inside themselves. They were withdrawn and inactive. When they were reunited they functioned better. They participated in classroom activities. They initiated behaviours with other kids. The yin–yang dichotomy was active while they were together and dysfunctional when apart.

From a Piagetian perspective, Lily and May Lee progressed from one cognitive stage to the next together in a sequential and simultaneous process. As toddlers they learned normally through sensory processing. Then they were normal concrete information processors and learned through reasoning with direct physical environmental influences. As they approached teen-age years and the ability to think abstractly they slowly started to differ. Both were diagnosed with anorexia nervosa at age thirteen. They were treated together. Initially, Lily did not show any greater improvements compared to May Lee. However, similar to many other identical twins, with increasing maturity levels they began to show some differences due to external influences and lifestyle choices. Lily decided to eat, May Lee did not. Nothing seemed to work with May Lee's thought processes. In her mind, May Lee thought she was morbidly obese and would not eat anything. Although Lily had issues with food and her body image, she ate and was no longer in any health risks or death danger. This was not the case for May Lee.

"I don't know what is wrong with May Lee," Lily explained. "I don't know why she will not eat. She must be hungry, but she is worried about her weight. She thinks she is too fat and needs to lose some more weight to be okay. She always wants to lose a little more weight."

It quickly became clear I was over my head with May Lee's psychological care. More importantly her physical health was rapidly deteriorating. One day, while I was on the Eating Disorders ward, May Lee was transferred to the Intensive Care Unit. Her body was shutting down. I continued to see Lily on an outpatient basis. Unlike May Lee, Lily was showing steady improvements with weight gain and increased self-esteem.

May Lee's death was inevitable. It came in the middle of the night. I received the telephone call early in the morning from the head nurse. When I arrived at the hospital to meet with the Chen family they were in the midst of making arrangements for the release of May Lee's body to the funeral home. It was a terribly tough time. Although they knew this was a likely outcome they always held hope May Lee would turn the corner and recover. I offered to help them with grief counselling or arrange an appropriate referral. The Chens graciously declined saying they have already put plans in place. Lily gave me a hug, and we said our goodbyes. That was it, the case was closed. We all moved on. A steep hill to climb for all of us, no doubt.

I successfully completed the internship at Children's Hospital. Throughout my time at the hospital I had some tough cases, pedestrian cases, and interesting cases, but none like the Chen sisters. Maybe it is more primacy effect than anything else; nevertheless, I will always remember May Lee and Lily. They taught me a lot and I am forever indebted for their instruction about sisters, twins, and anorexia culture.

I *graduated*. It was a nice sunny spring day in May. The cap and gown were dowdy, but the celebration was great. Russ bought a new suit. Colleen and Delia were dressed up in gorgeous spring attire. Michael made it over from Mill Bay. Maggie Westonmeyer cried from beginning to end, and for all I know, she is still crying. "I am so proud of you Karen," she said with a bone-crushing hug.

"Thanks Maggie," I said, "I couldn't have done it without your support and never ending love. You are the best friend in the world."

After the convocation ceremony we met at the Stanley Park Salmon House restaurant for dinner. It was a lovely time. I was happy. At one point I excused myself from the festivities to visit the restroom and freshen up. Along the way down the hall I glanced out the window and could see my daughter Delia sitting outside on a bench overlooking the bay. I went out to see her and say, "Hey, how you doing dear?"

"Great, thanks mum," she said smiling, "I am awfully proud of you. It is a great accomplishment. You did it!"

"Thanks."

"Do you still think about Jimmy," she asked.

"*Everyday*," I answered.

"Yeah, me too, I wish he was here today. He would have been so proud of you mum."

I blinked back any tears and said, "Yes, I know what you mean. But, in a way, he is here; he will always be with us. It is dull and daft, I know, but by envisioning him as ever present it gets me through the day. Your dad has religion, and I have a metaphysical image of Jimmy with me all the time. It doesn't always work well, but it is the best I can do. Otherwise, I would go nuts. Maybe I am nuts anyway. Who knows, you remember how Jimmy used to say, "The sun rises, the sun sets, a few things happen along the way, and that is it, that is the day."

Delia laughed, "We better get back to the table before they notice we are missing."

I agreed, looking over at the North Shore Mountains, "As Jimmy would probably say, pitter patter lets get at 'er." We held hands and walked back inside to join the party.

Miners Bay

Ms. Gabriella Antonella Rosabella Devanio, JD, had no sense whatsoever of interpersonal space perception. She was always coming way too close and getting right into my face, invading my personal space when I least expected such an intrusion. Maybe, and it is a slight maybe, it could have been my hypersensitive perception, but I don't think so. It is not as though Gabriella had some valid cultural background roots to cling to by way of a behavioural personality explanation, but I do. Sociologically, of course, I know that interpersonal spaces are culturally composed. A violation of space in one place is not in another. Gabriella does different things all the time. One just never knows what to expect from Gabriella.

Although I was born in Calgary, I spent some summers on my grandfather's farm in Southern Alberta during the "formative years." Talk about spaces, there were nothing but wide-open spaces, wheat fields, barley, flax, and grazing cows, too. Gramps did not want to put all the eggs in one basket. This was commonly called "mixed family farming" practices. Diversity was a wise thing to develop.

Just as much as I hold a rural heritage, Gabriella epitomizes the urban milieu. She was born in the Mount Royal neighbourhood of Montreal. Gabriella's parents had emigrated from Italy. I met them and their dozens of cousins just prior to our wedding. My side of the family was reasonably represented at the wedding, but we were definitely dominated by Devanios. And although to a neutral observer it sure sounded as though the Devanios were yelling and fighting with one another, I later learned this was just their preferred communication style. As much as we were introspective, quiet, contained, and cordial, the Devanios were not. Every family has their differences, I guess.

"Geez Gabbie, really, do you have to be so abrasive and condescending with the civilians?" I would ask.

As a lawyer Gabriella adhered to the successful strategy suggesting that the best defence is a good offence. She was a rising legal star. Gabriella's tough stance and aggressive strategies seemed to work for her. As a litigator, she was a winner, and for a lawyer, that was what it was all about. Nobody wants to hire a loser lawyer.

We want a winner. And, although he had a lot of horses, when Gramps went to the barn he always picked one of his best horses to do the job. He could have gone farther down the stalls and picked another less successful unaccomplished horse, but he always used his best most reliable to get the job done. Gabby's law firm worked that way, too.

For way, way too much modern money - good thing Grampa was gone - we bought an eight hundred and thirty-five square foot condominium on the twenty-third floor in a tower on one of Vancouver's busiest and trendiest intersections, Robson and Howe Street. Gabriella wanted to be closer to the firm's offices, which were on the forty-first to forty-fifth floors of the Royal Dominion Towers.

I did not particularly like living in a skyscraper. It felt like a human filing cabinet. We were filed away in our small space on the twenty-third floor. I often took the stairs, but I reluctantly used the elevator when I had groceries and sundries to carry. On the other hand, when we were living in the suburbs I sang Pete Seeger's ticky-tacky boxes suburb song.

Gabriella said there was no pleasing me. Neither downtown nor the suburbs seemed a comfortable fit, but we loved each other and adaptations were made. Mind you, when Gabriella wanted a divorce many of those earlier accommodations were forgotten and everything just turned rotten, nasty and sour.

Later Gabriella claimed the only reason she had stayed with me for as long as she did was because she suffers from an adult attachment disorder. That was according to her lawyer in a preliminary negotiating discussion with my lawyer, Mr. Dayton. However, the absolute truth—and the truth always comes out—was that I had become a *cuckold*. Gabriella had an affair with Donald Petersen, one of the firm's junior partners. Of course, Donnie was married with kids, but I guess these things happen in the big leagues. What would I know? As an accountant we work in different circles. Gabriella was weird that way.

"Dayton, eh," I said upon the first meeting with my Howe Street lawyer, "those guys make good boots."

He nodded with a small smile and confirmed that indeed the old Vancouver boot-making firm was part of his family background. I later learned, when his bill arrived, at four hundred and seventy-five dollars per hour, small talk adds up and runs up the bill. Pitter-patter just get at her was one of our old university mantras. It applied well in this case. I wish Jimmy Swanson were here. He always knew what to do. Jimmy knew how to handle things. He would not tolerate fools or basic bullshit. And this divorce was big bullshit.

Theoretically, this divorce was supposed to be simple. It was not, nothing is simple. We did not really have many assets, no kids, or pets to fight over their custody. My lawyer, Mr. Dayton, was a locally renowned expert and had recently won a very high profile divorce case involving Sophia the wiener dog. Her owners were divorcing and both spent way too much money on the custody battle for the dog. Who got the dog for Christmas went three rounds worth of court costs, legal fees, and disbursements.

Gabriella and I started quibbling and fighting—through our respective lawyers—over pieces of art, electrical appliances, and furniture. Some of the furniture was cheap and came from IKEA, too. Like many of these things the momentum starts slow and accelerates as the stupidity increases. Although my main lawyer's junior counsel, Ms. McGovern, tried to calm the pending storm. I had to start dealing with the junior lawyers because they were much, much cheaper. Every time Mr. Dayton had to talk on the telephone, dictates, or do anything, an invoiceable bill was generated, and that costs money. Once one understands the business of the divorce industry it is much easier to move along. "Okay, yes, of course, let's get this done."

However, having never done this before I was inept, inexperienced and uncomfortable. Fortunately, Ms. McGovern was patient as she explained that it was silly for us (me) to fight over used furniture and IKEA products. "Derek," she started in the most lawyer-like but counselling calm voice, "we will not gain much quibbling over pedestrian possessions. Remember, IKEA is just a Swedish acronym."

"Really, an acronym, I did not know that. What does it mean?"

Ms. McGovern was lovely. She looked good, professional, and was the epitome of patience. She knew we were wasting time, but educating me on trivial matters now may prove productive later. Besides, I was paying the bill. And the firm sent a bill regularly.

"The acronym IKEA comes from the founder *Ingvar Kamrad's* name, *Elmtaryd*—the farm where he grew up, and his hometown, *Agunnaryd* in South Sweden. Thus, IKEA is an acronym." Smiling, but showing some semblance of sternness, she suggested we push forward and get these issues drafted and filed "with the other side."

In the end, and there has to eventually be an endpoint, we finally settled on mutually agreeable terms and the divorce was decreed. Gabriella could keep the IKEA bookshelves, leather chesterfield, and Waterford dishes; I got the art from our working vacation in the Northwest Territories, and *all* the Tony Onley lithograph prints. The marriage was indeed over and it was now official. The court ordered it over and it was time to move on. Unlike the wedding ceremony, with all the relatives, friends, and fanfare, the divorce was quite quiet ending with us signing forms in our respective lawyer's offices. Mr.

Dayton was in court so Ms. McGovern and I signed the forms in the firm's oval office. And, as Jimmy would say: that was that—FIDO (Forget It Drive On).

Later that night I went out with my old buddies from our UBC days, crazy Craig Davidsen and Gerald Westonmeyer—Mike Lee got married and dropped away from many of our current antics. He was responsible and paced the events. You cannot do all of them all the time. First, we started out drinking basic beers at Darby's Pub and ended up drinking some sort of flaming shooters at Biminis.

The next morning my head hurt, but otherwise I was fine, moving on, and in the early stages of developing a new 'Plan Z.' I thought life would feel different, but I didn't. Much like when I was turning twenty-one the next day arrived and I felt nothing. I had a headache. It was the beginning of our tequila phase.

The more than way too expensive matrimonial condo asset had now sold, and although Gabriella initially tried to get a seventy to thirty percent split—in her favour—due to income discrepancies, down payment disbursements, and just because she felt she deserved it more than me, fell flat. However, she eventually acquiesced when pressed for palimony payments. We split fifty and fifty. It was fair and the papers were signed, sealed, and definitely delivered.

When we got back to my place, Gerald Westonmeyer worked me over way too hard, "Listen Derek, you have got to get off the fairness crap. Just play the cards you were dealt, and get on with it. Make a plan, put one foot in front of the other, keep up momentum and motivation and get out of this hole you have sunken into."

It was not fair. I did not want to be a cuckold. Maybe the deck was stacked. Maybe it was me after all. Certainly that was Gabriella's contention. In the end I realized that Wes was right. Perseverating on the facts did not change anything. The facts were the facts and no matter how the deck was cut, it was what it was, period. It was point, set, and match: I needed to regroup, and move on.

My buddy, Craig Davidsen suggested I take a vacation, and get re-organized. That was always his strategy. Whenever Davidsen was riding low in the saddle, he takes vacations, a leave of absence, sometimes he takes protracted sabbaticals, too. Turns out the cottage down the road from his mom's place on Mayne Island was up for rental. It was a good deal. I took it. Although, as personalities go, I am never impulsive, but these were different days, I had never been a cuckold before. Besides that, I never take Davidsen' frequently offered advice, either. But, that was then this was now, and moving on was a necessity. Well, at least I had to do something different because life with Gabriella was done, dead, detonated, and destroyed. I did not have much of a reason to stay in downtown Vancouver. Certainly did not want to return to the burbs, either.

The actual move was relatively easy. Gabriella had all my stuff packed into really nice boxes. It was a professional job. Turned out that Mayne Island was an ideal place for me to re-group, reorganize my life, and breathe really fresh air. Compared to Vancouver, or Montreal, Mayne Island was the complete representation of the fen shiu ying and yang of my previous residential existence. The condo where I lived with Gabriella was an expensive little box filed up high in the sky and swarming with people pushing and pulling me down the hall, and spilling out onto the busy urban street. My new place on Mayne Island was a cute cottage bungalow on the historic Miner's Bay beach. It was not deserted; there were some people around, but not very many. The road with potholes has some traffic, but not much.

The local general grocery store was reasonably within walking distance. And I was intent on doing more walking. The characters that ran the place were great, but the patrons were even better. Of course, everyone has a story. That is the same wherever you go, but these stories were attractive, interesting, and I was receptive. Even though I was just another city slicker descending to their part of the planet, I was well received. Everyone was excessively nice to me. But, that was just how it works there on the island. The regulars hate the weekenders, but I was deemed okay as a "new" resident with full-time status.

Elvirena, with the voice of a foghorn, probably from way too many cigarettes and red wine, ran the cash register. It seemed that she knew everything about eagles that there was to know, and then some.

I knew nothing, but after watching a pair nesting near my cottage, I became increasingly interested in these magnificent birds.

Ellie, as friends called her, and whose illustrious company I had invaded, explained that the pair of nesting eagles by my place was not new. "Those two eagles are like an old married couple," she explained as the cash register rang up my groceries. "They come back to the same nest year after year. They do some remodeling, but otherwise it is like clock work." Ellie went on to explain how eagles mate for life, returning to the same nest every year to hatch their eggs. "Their nests can weigh more than a tonne."

Monogamy and eagles, eh? Great, glad to hear it, I thought to myself as I unloaded groceries into the cottage's refrigerator and pantry. Looking out the large kitchen window I could see the eagles swooping by the bay on their way to the grove of Arbutus trees where they perched. Just then the old landline wall mounted telephone with a long curly cord started ringing, I picked it up to hear, "Hey Derek, how you doing?" Craig Davidsen asked.

"Hello Craig" I replied with a smirk, "I'm doing fine, thanks."

"Yeah well the last time I saw you the song you were singing was: I am younger than I act, but older than I look."

"It's a Jesse Winchester song," I replied. "Yankee Lady, draft dodger, c'mon."

"Never heard of him," Davidsen said dismissively.

I can spar too, "Coming from the guy who was caught *in flagrante delicto* with Breanne Lacroix from Pouce Coupe, you should talk, eh."

Even on the old landline telephone, I could see him wince.

"And Derek delivers a low blow," Davidsen countered with exasperated tones. "I cannot believe how word gets around."

"Yeah, well I can't believe you hooked up with Bree, doing the wild thing in her parents' ranch house."

Davidsen sighed, "Oh well, these things just sort of happen. I really felt bad about getting caught in bed by her Papa. We thought we were home alone, one thing led to another and we were horizontal, but then her Papa pops in to say Bonjour."

"Oh man, you are an idiot!"

"Takes one to know one."

"You going back to Pouce Coupe soon, or are you banished?"

Davidsen did his familiar lip-purring low groan, "No, I am not banished, but not going back for a while either. Actually, my sister and I are coming over to Mayne this weekend for my mum's birthday party. That is why I am calling you now. Do you see my mum around the island much?"

"Awe nah, I keep to myself, but yes, sure is a small island with like a thousand people or so. Naturally, I see Janice around. She has a lot of friends and doesn't need me bugging her about you and your issues."

"Issues, oh man, Gabby Devanio says you have more issues real and imagined than anyone!"

"You are *not* seeing my ex-wife are you?"

"No, just pushing your buttons man. The Gabster is a goof. I'd never ever get involved with a goof. And if I needed a lawyer, it would not be *her*!"

That was the final straw. He was pushing my buttons eh? I was ready to blast him both barrels, and then there is a tapping on my front window. Glancing over I see none other than the most lovely Mrs. Janice Davidsen, Craig's mum, holding a plate of Nanaimo bars, waving and pointing to the door to let her in.

· I let the phone dangle and went to open the door, "Hi Mrs. Davidsen, come in please, you would not believe who is on the telephone."

"Oh Derek, don't let me disturb you. We can talk later when you are not busy."

Handing her the telephone receiver, I said, "Here, talk some sense into this guy, will ya.

"Hello, is that you Craig? Yes, I am over visiting Derek to invite him to the party on Saturday just in case you forgot. People do not plan to fail they fail to make plans. Derek is doing a lot of planning over here on Mayne." she said with a wink and a smile in my direction.

They exchanged some mother – son pleasantries and before hanging up the phone Mrs. D. asked, "Are you finished with Craig?"

"Yes, thanks, just tell him I will see everyone on Saturday. Maybe we can go kayaking in the morning?"

Kayaking was an inside joke. Davidsen never told his mum about his mishap and near drowning episode off Curlew Island during his previous visit to Mayne. But I knew, and never planned to let him live it down. What an idiot.

I was told, "Come to the birthday party at six on Saturday." I strolled over around 6:30 and the place was hopping. Cars were parked everywhere in a haphazard fashion, music was blasting with people milling about on the deck, in the house, and front yard. Davidsen and his sister Debbie arrived a couple of hours earlier. Ferry issues prevented an earlier rendezvous.

Mrs. Davidsen runs with the Mayne Library volunteer crowd and coffee klatch group. You got to love middle-aged folks - they are a different group altogether. "Hi Derek," Mrs. D hollered as I approached the house, "come and meet your neighbours." Yes, I knew that, on Mayne everyone on the whole island was considered "your neighbour."

Debbie planted a kiss on my cheek with a strong hug. "Hi Derek, great to see you. Mum says you are settled and doing well here on Mayne."

"Yes, thanks Deb, nice to see you, too. Your mum is correct, it's great, and I really like life here on Mayne. How's your dorky brother doing?

"Oh you know Craig," she said with a smile, "It's not easy acting crazy all the time eh? What can *you* tell me about Breanne Lacroix and my brother? What happened in Pouce Coupe?"

"Oh Deb, what happened was nothing you likely do not know already. Speak of the devil."

Debbie's baby brother, and my crazy cousin, Craig, approached us and tried to put me in a headlock - his way of saying hello. However, I foiled him with a spin about move reverse half-Nelson maneuver. "Hello to you too," I said. He was now trapped, "Say Uncle and I will let you go."

Dumb old Davidsen squirmed, trying to break free, but it was no use. He had to say it.

"Okay, ok, uncle."

I released my hold. "Craig, remember, play with the bull, you will get the horn."

Dusting himself off, the only reply he could offer was, "Butt wipe."

Debbie excused herself saying, "You two are too juvenile for me. I am going to mingle."

Davidsen delivered a "Yes, Deborah, you are only young *once*, but you can be immature *forever*!"

"No probs Deb," I said "good turnout for your mum's party. Please, go mingle on our behalf, too. Lots of white heads here."

Scoffing with a smile, "Oh yeah, you got that right Derek."

I enjoyed the party. The food was overwhelming! Those Mayne Islanders turn out great grub, and in large quantities, too. The after-party ended up back at my place. Davidsen talked sister Debbie into trying flaming shooters. I stuck to basic beer. Didn't matter, I ended up drunk dialing Breanne Lacroix. Passing the phone over to Davidsen was the debacle. He is an idiot.

"Bree, listen, sorry about how things turned out," Davidsen started his diatribe. "Morson and my sister Debbie are telling me that I should return to Pouce Coupe and patch things up with your papa."

With a voice of a sea lion, Debbie squawked, "Craig, you LIE-OH, I said no such thing Bree. Don't listen to him. He lies!"

Bree's tolerance diminished as Davidsen's blubbering increased. Finally, in exasperation, "Craig, call me tomorrow when you make more sense. Good night!" and she hung up on him.

Shaking his head in disbelief, Davidsen moaned, "She hung up on me. Oh man, can you believe that? She hung up on me."

Debbie, who also had more than enough beverages, but knew her limit, snatched the phone from him, "Leave her alone Craig. You've done enough. Call tomorrow!"

It was getting late and the after-party had run its course. Deb gave me a peck-kiss on the cheek to say good-bye. She gathered her stuff, including her drunken brother, and cleared out in a flash.

Stumbling off to bed I shut down the place for the evening. I made sure everything was turned off that needed to be turned off. Safety first. Primitive electrical wiring always makes me nervous. My head hit the pillow and sleep came quickly.

I woke to hear voices and digging noises outside the back of the cottage. The sun was streaming through the window and the clock read 9:15. It seemed early to me for someone to be working on a Sunday morning. Sliding open the curtains I could see Mrs. Davidsen, another lady, and some twenty-somethings digging and milling about the back yard.

Fine by me, no worries here, I was just going to go back to bed. Too late, Mrs. D saw me at the window and started waving. "Good morning Derek, come on out, I want to introduce you to the Tanaka family."

Certainly, as my crazy cousin Craig is a bona fide idiot, Mrs. D is the antithesis. Historically, they both seem to get themselves into complicated situations. For the most part, Craig gets into pejorative positions while his mum gets into positive productions.

I got quasi-dressed slipping on SeaWheeze flip-flops, shorts and a light mackinaw shirt. Wiping the sleep from my eyes, dealing with Mrs. D's heavy hug greeting, and my hurting head, "Good morning," was about the best I could come up with by way of salutations. "Great party yesterday Mrs. D." While I had no hugs for new people, I just held out my hand. "Hi, I'm Derek Morson, nice to meet you."

Mrs. D started the intros to her new acquaintances and accomplices. "Derek, this is Judy Tanaka, her husband Tosh, son Glen, and daughter Marie."

"Hey, whats up, you digging for buried treasure?" was my lame retort, but seriously, I was still suffering from morning wonkiness, only functioning on a couple of cylinders, and partially hung over. Just think how Craig feels.

Mrs. D had met the Tanaka family while working at the Mayne Island library. They had come into the library looking for archival maps and census information. Mrs. D explained that the old house where I was now living had once been the home of a Japanese–Canadian family. Although Judy Tanaka had been born in a Slocan Valley internment camp for Japanese in June 1943, she believed this might be the house where her parents and older brother, Kiyoshi, once lived.

Mayne Island once had a thriving community of Japanese settlers. The house up the road, now a restaurant, was originally built in 1910. Kumazo Nagata bought the house in 1921 and then enlarged it in 1937. Judy Tanaka's parents and Nagata family built green houses where they grew tomatoes. Mayne Island was once very famous for their fine tomatoes.

Everything quickly changed after the "Day of Infamy" December 7, 1941 attack on Pearl Harbour. Three hundred and fifty three Japanese fighter airplanes, bombers, and torpedo planes came in two waves to attack the American fleet stationed at Pearl Harbour. The Japanese attack was completely unexpected and killed over two thousand Americans. Shortly thereafter the USA entered World War Two. And the world was never the same again.

The Dominion of Canada (we were still a satellite of England's British Empire, and did not get a constitution until 1982) was already too well immersed in the war. However, after Pearl Harbour, the Canadian Prime Minister, William Lyon Mackenzie King, invoked the War Measures Act. This Act interned (gaoled, jailed, incarcerated) over twenty-three thousand (23,000) Japanese-Canadians and Japanese nationals. Some were sent to camps in the interior. Some were sent to work on sugar beet farms. All Japanese nationals and Japanese-Canadians were removed from the West Coast. Mayne Island was not exempt.

Mrs. D explained that Judy Tanaka was born in the Slocan internment camp. The Slocan camp was located in the BC interior region of West Kootenay. The name Slocan came from the Sinixt First Nations meaning to hit or pierce the head. It was from their salmon harpoon heritage. There were other internment camps scattered throughout the interior.

With a stern expression Mrs. D described that "On Tuesday, April 21, 1942, the Canadian Pacific Railroad's steamship *Princess Mary* arrived at the Mayne Island Miners Bay wharf to collect the fifty Japanese men, women and children who were patiently waiting to be taken away to the internment camp. Judy's parents and older brother were whisked away. They were sad to leave as quickly as were many of their neighbours who were there on the dock to say fare thee well."

The Tanakas were forced to leave quickly and were not allowed to take many possessions with them to the internment camp. Consequently, they and many others buried bottles of home brewed sake, and other personal belongings throughout the island. At x-mas they would write letters to their white neighbours instructing where to dig to find a buried gift of sake.

"Derek, get this," Mrs. D explained, "Judy was born in the same internment camp as David Suzuki."

"Actually Janice," Judy began to clarify, "David was born in Vancouver in 1936. True, we lived in the same camp, but he is seven years older than me. He might have played baseball with my brother Gordon Kiyoshi, but I was too little, and a girl."

We all chuckled at the idea.

Shaking her head with disgust, Janice volleyed, "Can you believe David Suzuki was born in Vancouver, but was sent to an internment camp? Now he is a revered and celebrated citizen. And, Ken Adachi was also born in Vancouver, interned in Slocan, too. In the library we have Adachi's book, *The enemy that never was.*"

"Adachi, wasn't he the Toronto writer who committed suicide at age sixty?" I asked.

"WoW, Derek, that is pretty random, where did you get that tidbit?" Mrs. D asked.

"UBC undergrad literature," I replied. "I wrote a term paper on writers who committed suicide at age sixty. Adachi and Hemmingway were on the list."

Judy joined in saying, "Yes, Ken was way older. He was born in 1929. My husband Tosh knows his family in Toronto. It was a shame to hear of his suicide. I did not know him personally, but he lived in the Slocan camp when we were there."

Tosh, who had just kept quietly digging all the while we were chit chatting, looked up, nodded his head, and kept digging.

"Oh Derek, by the way," Mrs. D continued, "I took the liberty of telling the Tanakas that I knew who lived in this house and I was sure you would not mind us digging around."

"Course not," I replied. "Just a sec, I'm going to the tool shed, get a shovel and help out instead of standing here like an oaf."

The Tanakas were following a lead that suggested prior to their family's sudden internment they and other Mayne Island relatives had buried various items at this location. Tosh was showing his son Glen, and daughter Marie, where to systematically dig.

Some months ago when Judy's mother, Umiko Tanaka passed away at the ripe old age of 93, the family found a batch of letters and documents in a box marked "Mayne Island." It was through the process of probate, and fulfilling her last wishes that they learned the urn containing Umiko's stillborn baby was buried along with other items that they could not take to the internment camp. Upon her death Umiko wanted to be reunited with her stillborn boy. She wanted his urn placed by her in the family plot in Taber.

Of course, I did not know about the baby until much later. I thought we were digging for Sake, and we were, but Marie explained they were looking for her uncle (stillborn baby boy).

Hard for me to estimate Marie Tanaka's age, as a math-man I knew Judy Tanaka was born in the Slocan internment camp in 1943 or 1944. That would place her age at late sixty something—but she looked younger. Thus, Marie, her youngest child might be twenty something, but could be in her early thirties. At any rate, however you calculate, Marie was gorgeous. Medium height, sorta slight, but not too thin. Long black hair tied back in a ponytail, and clear beautiful almond coloured eyes that seemed to smile with her glance my way. It was the eye contact that made me dizzy.

Okay, ok, I know, I am bad that way, but oh man, Marie Tanaka's smile made the digging worthwhile. Although her father, Tosh, seemed to think we were systematically digging in a grid fashion, I had some doubts and we had not found anything of note since starting.

Gabbie would never get her hands dirty with real earthen dirt. As a lawyer, she did not hesitate to play dirty, sling mud, but she can't break a nail, either. Manicures were an important profile point. Gabby dislikes people with bad nails (female and male). Let's not get started on nail biters either.

Yes, yes, yes, I know I should not waste any of my brain cells or a nano second thinking about Gabbie, her foibles and idiotic projections. Guess it was because Marie Tanaka was the polar opposite in so many ways that I made the comparison.

Mrs. D says, "Give it time Derek. These things take time."

Oh the time thing, eh. Yes, I have heard that before. How much time? Although Craig says I am a random thinker, I think I am a linear thinker. Where is the beginning and where is the end? If I can measure it and pace it out I can understand. When crazy Jimmy Swanson talked us all into running the Vancouver Marathon it was long and grueling, but we did it. Measurement-wise it did not matter whether you were a miles man or a kilometre person. They had signs throughout the whole route marking the distance we had travelled and how far we had to go. We all finished. I had a good time, not a fast time; it was a good (happy) time (3:47). Michael Lee (3:22) beat us all. The guy was a maniac.

For the most part our old college crew were compatible, copacetic, cooperative and not all that competitive with each other. The world was different back then. Jimmy was a ringleader in some ways, Mikey was the brains in the group, Morgan was practical, Gerald was funny, and Craig always had ups and downs, but he was all right.

When Jimmy died nothing was ever the same with our gang. You cannot drive a car without an engine. I really, really miss Jimmy.

Glancing over at Marie I realized that it's embarrassing to feel this way. Why do I do it? I do not know. And then Marie smiles at me again. Gawd she is gorgeous. Just then my shovel hit something. "Whoa folks I got something here!" I called.

Tosh came over, politely asked, "May I have a look Derek?"

Moving out of the way to let Tosh take over, I said, "Yeah man, I'm a hack, and know nothing about archeology and midden digs."

Glen and Marie dropped their shovels and came over to check out what I had discovered. Marie put her hand on my shoulder. Maybe it was for stability purposes, but whatever, I shivered on the inside with a tingle, too. It seemed as though she sorta snuggled into me.

Earlier Glen had uncovered a disintegrating wooden box of Sake, but this was something different, a metal box or something. Tosh carefully dug around the periphery of what was to turn out as an old steamer trunk. It was sturdy, heavy, and in remarkably good condition.

"Derek," Tosh grunted, "Could you give me a hand with this end, please."

Together Tosh and I gave it the old heave ho and out you go from its buried resting spot. It was a black metal brass fittings steamer trunk. We wrestled it out in to the open area.

While brushing off the front of the trunk, Glen Tanaka noted, "Dad, looks like you may need a key for this lock on the front."

True enough, the trunk was locked or sealed shut through the ides of time. "Dad, is it ethical to try and pick the lock of a trunk that does not belong to us?" Marie asked.

"How do you know it does not belong to us?" Glen asked. "Perhaps this trunk belonged to Grandmother Tanaka and that would make it ours through succession principles."

Me, as Einstein's longstanding protégé, I suggested, "Let's look and see if there is a name on it somewhere."

"Good idea," Marie, my most marvelous maven concurred. "Check it out dad, maybe there is a name somewhere."

No name on the outside or if there once was it is gone now. Opening the trunk was our next endeavour. The slight pry try at the top was unsuccessful. We pried harder with no luck. Picking the lock was not working either.

"Well, folks, there is a crowbar in the tool shed. Should we give it a try?" I asked.

Tosh nodded, "Yes, I think that will work."

Indeed, I returned with a rusty old crowbar, Tosh positioned the claw in place, gave it some muscle and the latch popped open.

We all sort of held our collective breath with anticipation as Tosh open the trunk's lid. The top layer was a type of shelf with linens, clothes, and doily type things.

Marie held out a bag, "Dad, let's put some of those in here."

Next, Tosh lifted out the shelf revealing dishes, vases, and finally, the urn they had come in search of. "This is it," Tosh spoke softly handing the urn to Glen.

Marie started crying.

Janice D started humming to fill the space, out of nervousness, I guess.

Glen handed the urn to his mother.

The emotions and gravity of the moment were contagious. I lightly placed my hand on Marie's back—it was quite appropriate, comforting, and not untoward in any way. She turned her head to me with a serious look, and softly said, "Thanks Derek."

The urn was not as big as I thought it would be. It was a reddish colour with Japanese characters on the side. And it was now reunited with its ancestors.

"Well, what a morning this has been," Mrs. D said. "Would you all like to come up to my place for lunch?" She nodded for everyone's behalf. "I am so glad your search has been successful. This urn is where it belongs—back with family. Judy you can take your brother's ashes home."

"Yes, thank you Janice. We could not have done this without your help."

"Oh, well, I don't know about that, but we were lucky the library had archival maps and documents on file, is all I can say."

I went inside, showered, shaved, and got ready for lunch. Fussed for fifteen minutes over which shirt to wear: black, blue, white, madras, collar, sleeves—long or short. If Jimmy were looking over my shoulder this would not go over well. So I stopped and just went with a T-shirt and denim.

When I arrived for lunch Mrs. D and daughter Deb were buzzing about getting things on the table. Craig had recently rolled out of bed and was no help whatsoever. If anything he was getting in the way by sampling food faster than they could put it on the table. They planned on catching the late night ferry.

The Tanakas were scattered around the place checking things out before lunch was served. I found Marie standing on the deck overlooking Miners Bay.

"Hi Derek," Marie smiled and waved me over. "What a view from here, eh?"

"Yes, this lighting on the water is something else. I love trying to figure out if the tide is coming in or going out." I said with a panoramic gesture. "But, hey, on a serious note, how you doing? Glad we were able to find your uncle's urn."

She smiled, touched me on the arm, and said, "Yes, thanks Derek, my parents feel a great relief."

"How about you?" I asked. "How are you doing?"

She gave my arm a squeeze, smiled, and said, "Yes, it is a huge relief for the whole family. We can honour grandmother's wish."

"When are you going home?" I asked.

"I'll be back in L.A. on Wednesday. First flying to Calgary and then driving the two hours home."

At first I thought she meant Los Angeles, California. However, she smiled, again, saying, "Lethbridge, Alberta is where we live Derek."

Marie went on to explain, under the auspices of a heads up. It was as though she seemed to know it was likely a good idea to give me a cognitive advanced organizer to ensure a reasoned response on my part. Her parents were planning to invite Mrs. D and me to attend their family ceremony where the urn was going to be placed along side Umiko Tanaka.

Prior to today I always thought L.A. was California, now I think of L.A. as Lethbridge, Alberta. Prior to today I never heard of a columbarium nor did I know about cinerary urns, either. Learned a lot today.

Just as Marie had forewarned, her father stood up during the lunch and made a formal request asking Mrs. D and me to join them in Lethbridge to fulfill Umiko Tanaka's final wishes.

Mrs. D looked at me. I gave the thumbs up sign. And there you go a road trip was on. We were going to Lethbridge. I knew not where it was or how to get there, but it was on.

Before leaving, Marie asked for my email address and or phone number so she could give me more details as they developed in the next few days. "Derek, this is one of my business cards," she said gently placing the white embossed card in my hand. "It has my email, fax, and office numbers. Here, I will write my cell number on the back."

"Great, thanks Marie," I said reading the card out loud, "Dr. Marie Tanaka, MD, Cardiology, Lethbridge General Hospital."

She smiled and said, "Okay, see you soon." And with that Marie gave me a big hug, kiss on the cheek, slight release, and then another kiss in the middle of my forehead.

Out of the corner of my eye I saw Mrs. D holding up a similar card and giving me the thumbs up signal.

Oh-man, oh-man, what a road trip it will be with Mrs. D.

Crazy Cousins Other Side

Westonmeyer always follows me. We were lost and we knew it. It was an accepted fact. He just wanted to sit still and *wait* for help to find us. Unlike Gerald, I am proactive, autonomous, independent, and it was my mistake to repair. I wanted to walk out on my own without rescue assistance. Gerry waits for the world to catch up to him. I am not all that dominant, but I chase the world, I am not waiting around.

Gerald always thinks there will be someone to bail him out. Often I am the one who bails him out of whatever mishap he has created. But, he is my cousin, and I am duty bound due to bloodline. Bailing him out is what I do. He is the craziest cousin. The rest are okay, but Gerry, he has always been different.

You can lead a horse to water, you cannot make him drink.

What was I to do? Buddha-baby already, we were Zeusified. Gerald was just sitting on the stupid stone saying we must stay and wait for help to find us. Waiting was not my choice. I had evening obligations. There was a family soirée dinner that required my attendance by 7:00. I knew if I could find the trail out there was still enough time to make it to dinner. Or, I would at minimum be fashionably late.

I kept thinking he would get up and follow me out. The last thing I remember my cousin Gerald saying was, "C'mon Jimmy, just sit down, and let's figure this out."

There was nothing to "figure out." We were lost and needed to get moving. What an accountant, figure it out. He could not see the forest for the trees.

Gerald was always that way and he will never change. When we were kids we ruled the world. We rode our bikes everywhere. Nowhere was ever too far back then. One time, when we were thirteen, we rode our bikes all the way to Science World. Gerald was all stoked-up about the new featured exhibit - which I cannot remember the theme of now, but he was excited. He should have been a scientist.

Derek Morson, Craig Davidsen, Gerry, and I all met at the house on Canarvon Street. We rode an easy ride to the Science World dome. As a quartet we travelled well. Two duets were common, too.

Davidsen and Morson locked their bikes together. Gerry and I locked ours together. We always did it that way. Probably done it that way a hundred times or so. But, this time things went south.

After a few hours of Science World exhibits and activities it was time to go home. Spirits were high and a good time was had by all, that is until we returned to the bikes. Gerry's bike was gone. His front wheel was left locked to my bike. It was simple to "figure out."

In his exuberance to get inside Science World quickly Gerald had locked his bike to mine, but he neglected to realize that the quick release front wheel on his new red Rocky Mountain Hammer bike made it vulnerable to thieves. Mine was fine. It was securely locked to the pole. The thieves simply snapped off Gerry's quick release front wheel and took the rest of the bike. They could steal another front wheel elsewhere. Presto, thieves had a nice bike now.

He was bummed out big time. It was a mistake. We all make mistakes. Gerry unlocked his front wheel from my bike and began tromping home in a mood. It was a long way home by foot. For a while we all rode beside him and offered various suggestions from taking a bus to getting Derek's mum to come pick us up in the mini van. He was in a mood and not consolable. Told us to take off and wanted to walk home on his own.

I phoned him later that night. Mrs. Westonmeyer said, "Gerry has gone to bed, but you should call back tomorrow Jimmy."

WoW what a coping mechanism, the kid was a sleeper. He just sleeps it off. The next day he was tapping on my bedroom window too soon after dawn. I opened the curtains and there was my crazy cousin Gerry smiling ear to ear. His dad had said, "Don't sweat the small stuff, we have insurance. You can get a new bike."

There was Gerry with a sweeping motion showing me his new black Brodie bike. "Let's get the guys and go riding!"

On the other hand, Breanne, my ex-girlfriend, former girlfriend, whatever, (but don't call her my "partner" because she is overly sensitive and reacts to the term partner, poorly). Unlike Gerry, Breanne will stay awake all night tossing and turning, moaning and groaning about a problem. Cognitive compartmentalization is her Achilles. Just shake it off for a while, tomorrow comes soon enough, why fuss tonight. Let's get some sleep.

Breanne wanted to get married, and I did not. We went ten rounds over that issue. No one won that bout because we broke up over the issue—a lose, lose situation. Ultimately her ultimatum did us in and detonated the whole deal to pieces. And that was really too bad because I thought we had a good thing going.

It was getting darker. I thought I heard footsteps and held out hope that Gerry had caught up to me. I stopped to listen and see if it really was Gerry, but it wasn't. The darkening dusk was playing tricks on me. I was calm, but getting more and more concerned about the situation. Stay calm and carry on—oh those Brits and their mottos are not helping me now.

Fear is a funny feeling. Scared seems silly at this point, but I was wavering. Maybe I should have stayed with Gerald. Now I was really lost and had no idea of where I was or worse yet, where I was going.

I had no choice other than to keep on ploughing ahead in what I thought was the right direction.

Finally, after what seemed an eternity of anxiety and angst, I saw some light up a head. Phew, whew wee, I felt a great sense of relief. However, I was wrong, and I realized my mistake as I began falling. The first slip of my foot gave me a startle. And then everything started going down in slow motion. I was falling off the edge of the mountain. Just sort of flailed around in the air, no tricks, no half gainer or pike position. I had simply walked off the side of the mountain. I landed on a rocky ledge some ninety metres below.

And that was that.

Acknowledgements

In my previous novel, *Cape Lazo,* many people read autobiographical, biographical, and socio-political sentiments into the text, that book and this one are both fiction.

Having said that, however, there are people and places that influenced this book, and this is the appropriate place to acknowledge their contribution. If I accidently inadvertently leave anyone off this list, please forgive me, and I will put you in the next one when it is finished.

November 1969, my good buddy, Ronald Weston Widmeyer, was able to help get me a job working as a ski-lift operator at Snowridge Ski Resort in the Kananaskis Mountain range. My previous job was a truck driver; the ski resort was less pay, but less stress, too. One night mid-December Ron and I decided to drive into Banff for an evening of fun and relaxation. We did not know the gas gauge in the car was defective. We were in the middle of nowhere when we ran out of gas. The walk back to the ski resort was definitely way too far, but the walk to the highway junction was awfully far, too. It was terribly cold outside in the mountain pass. We did not want to stay and wait in the car. We got started walking when I suggested a short cut I had seen on a previous sojourn to Banff. I was positive we could get to the main highway by taking the "short cut." It was a bit of a debate. I knew we could not sit and wait for a rescue car to pick us up as there would be no traffic until morning when the ski resort opened. However, the short cut clearly was not a good idea, but we just did not know it at the time. Fortunately Ron's persuasion won over and we followed his instincts to stay on the original path. Eventually we made it to the highway junction where we flagged down a passing car to take us to the gas station down the road. We made it through the night to the next morning, retrieved the car, gassed it up, and went to work.

Innisfail Bob (Innisfail a small town in central Alberta named from an Irish epithet Isle of Destiny), who knew the Kananaskis trail area well explained my short cut, would have been a fatal choice. Lucky I guess, good choice to follow Ron's instincts. Hence the germination and general idea for the story/chapter Crazy Cousins originated on that cold mountain road. My sense of direction has never been very good.

In this book Jimmy Swanson, and others, sometimes say, "Pitter patter, lets get at 'er." Over a large number of years many of my UBC students have been heard to utter the pitter-patter slogan. I proliferate it, but did not originate it.

In the summer of 1972, Calgary's Captain (ret.) Norman Peter Christopher Zimmer and I had a roof-clip business. It did not take too long and our small business went bust. The machinery kept breaking down and our productivity was not paying the rent. We quickly got jobs working on a mobile home assembly line (although I love summer just could not wait for September to get back to college). Norm and I commuted to the assembly line plant in his 1968 Triumph 250. My bug eyed Sprite was less than reliable. That summer during roof-clip coffee breaks and/or commuting renditions the phrase became ingrained. Whether Norm or his lovely mother, Natalie, invented the phrase, I do not know, but still utilize accordingly.

January 1974, Susan Smith Dinning, Ronald S. Dinning and I rented the top floor of a house on Spaulding Street (just down the road from where Dr. Timothy Leary lived when he earned a Masters degree at WSU). Although I had three perfect pair of Seafarer jeans (cf. Don Henley), Susan and I would periodically frequent the Pullman laundromat (cell phone and text messages were yet to be invented, when the laundry was done we simply put a dime in the phone box ala Jim Croce and called Ron for pickup). It was while we watched the dryers spinning that Susan gave me the neurological compass concept that I use in Crazy Cousins. One of the Smiths (there is a lot of them) could be blindfolded, spun around a bunch of times, and then still correctly identify directionality. I come from a family of left-handers who cannot do those things. In addition to all Susan taught me about bacteriology, I remain indebted to the neurological compass concept.

January 1978, one of the best positions I have ever held was working with Dr. Gordon K. Hirabayashi as a Social Psychology Teaching Assistant at the University of Alberta. Gordon got me a terrific office in the Small Groups Laboratory. We held regular staff meetings in either his office or mine. I never drank coffee until then. During our staff meetings we did talk about social psychology (my favourite branch of psychology—just too hard to earn a living on that limb), but it was Gordon's description of his experience during World War Two that popped my eyes out.

When Gordon was a student at the University of Washington the Japanese attacked Pearl Harbour. Certainly, at the time, Gordon knew this was a terrible tragedy. Little did he know at that time the personal magnitude it would toll.

Gordon was born in Seattle. He graduated from Auburn High School. He was as all American as they come. A self-defined "sports nut." We played on the Sociology Department's pickup basketball team. Gordon was a formidable defensive player and a good shot, too.

Gordon explained how dumbfounded he felt when the Japanese-American internment was announced. At first he did not think it actually applied to him personally. He was born in Seattle—an American.

Gordon Kiyoshi Hirabayashi (April 23, 1918 to January 2, 2012) did a lot of things in his life. One of the most notable was his principled stand against internment. For that he spent time in prison.

In 1987 Gordon's conviction was overturned by the Court of Appeals for the Ninth Circuit.

John D. Carter

In 2012 President Barack Obama announced Gordon Hirabayashi would receive the Presidential Medal of Freedom for his stand against Japanese-American internment. The President presented the award posthumously to Gordon's family.

To me, Gordon was a great mentor. He was a big help on my master's thesis. Gordon always said, "The best thesis is a completed thesis."

Basil Stuart-Stubbs (1930 – 2012) was the UBC Head Librarian from 1964 to 1981. Basil regularly ran library orientations for new staff members. In the fall of 1975 I was hired as a Stack Attendant at the UBC Main Library.

I had the good fortune to experience one of Basil's library orientations.

In this book the chapter/story called *Metaphoric Mountains* describes Basil Stuart-Stubbs library tours. "Anything you want to know about anything we will have it inside this library. And if by some chance we do not have the specific title the patron is searching, we will get it through Interlibrary Loans," is a direct quote. I hear his voice today.

It was a sunny September day when Basil took us outside in front of the library to show us the sculptures/gargoyles of the monkey holding a scroll to show architectural solidarity with the Scopes teacher trail.

The following year, September 1976, I began a three-decade relationship with the UBC Law Library. Although I only worked a total of five years at the Law Library, my friends, Allen Soroka, Thomas Shorthouse, and Frances Wong, always gave me back my old job or another whenever I asked.

It was the fall of 1976 when I met Beverly McLachlin who was a UBC Law Professor at that time. Prof. McLachlin spent a lot of time in the Faculty Law Library room (the internet, quicklaw, lexis nexis were not invented, yet). My job involved shelving, retrieving, and maintaining the Faculty Law Library room, along with some other library tasks. Bev was always quick with a quip, friendly with a smile, and most appreciative of any assistance in locating esoteric and basic missing law reports, journals, and monographs (if I could not find it Frances could). Little did we know, at that time, that Bev would go on and become the Chief Judge of Canada's Supreme Court.

It was in late 2002 that the Supreme Court of Canada overturned the decision to ban books showing same-sex relationships in Surrey schools. Chief Justice Beverly McLachlin ruled that a school board could not impose their religious values and bans the books *One Dad, Two Dads, Brown Dads, Blue Dads*.

Tennessee had the teacher John Scopes who taught evolution. British Columbia had James Chamberlain who taught literature. Although Basil Stuart-Stubbs has passed on, I am sure he would agree that new gargoyle/sculptures would be warranted on the new library wing.

In the story/chapter one, *The Accountant's Girlfriend*, I note that the BC Lions have won six (6) Grey Cup Championships, but the Vancouver Canucks have played in four (4) Stanley Cup series never to win. Although this is true, it is through no fault of Daniel and/or Henrik Sedin. They are both excellent hockey players, sports statesmen, and the best "ambassadors" Sweden could ever send our way (I have Norwegian ancestors). Who knows how much longer the Sedins will play in Vancouver? They have already contributed a lot since their first season in 2000 - 2001 (two President's trophies and two scoring titles—Henrik was the Art Ross winner 2010, Daniel in 2011).

June 10, 2012, I met Daniel Sedin (I had a fifty-fifty chance of correct guessing but due to the fact that he was wearing a t-shirt, shorts, and flip-flops with a banged up foot injury I guessed Daniel not Henrik) in the checkout line-up at the Kitsilano Whole Foods grocery store.

Although in greater Vancouver the Sedins are hockey heroes, no one in the long line up seemed to know who he was or if they did were too polite to say anything. Myself, an expert in "small talk" and standing right beside him had to ask, "So what do you think will happen in tomorrow's game?" I was referring to the next day's game six Stanley Cup final.

Happy to engage in grocery store line-up hockey talk, Mr Sedin replied, "I think LA has a good chance because Jonathan Quick has been so good, but you can never count Jersey out."

I followed with some other quip about Quick. And the grocery line moved on. My niece Charlotte was disappointed I did not take his picture with my ever-present iPhone. But I did not want to impose and was happy he spoke with me at any rate. I hope the Sedins win a Stanley Cup before retirement.

Michael Louie, MBA, CA, was a big help in getting this book off the ground. Prior to writing *Crazy Cousins* I did not know the difference between a General Certified Accountant (GCA) and a Chartered Accountant (CA). Both groups seemed pervasive in the BC accounting landscape. Michael and I exchanged some emails. With statesmanlike neutrality Michael sent some urls so I could examine the criteria and qualifications for respective titles. Although Michael was a big help, he bears no responsibility for any miscalculations or accounting errors in the book. Any errors are mine.

Dr. Barbara Holmes and I have run countless road races (8 km, 10 km, half marathons, and the Vancouver Marathon). The races were fine, but it was the training that took time. Barbara's never ending encouragement through the rain, sleet, and snow, always made me feel good to get up and go. After reading an early draft of *Crazy Cousins* Barbara offered a familiar phrase: you have to finish it.

Delia is the name of the town where Enid Olive grew up. Hence it seemed like a good name for an attractive crazy cousin character.

Patti Weiss proofread this book. Although Patti encouraged me to retain an editor, Lee Swanson, my doctoral dissertation supervisor, would agree that my writing and speech patterns could be little more linear. John Lennon, Paul McCartney wrote it, Ringo sang lead, "I get by with a little help from my friends." Indeed, I remain indebted to my friends who helped me with this book.

Allen Soroka (1986) says, "If it's true they cannot sue. Just check Fleming on torts."

Ron Dinning (The Sloggs – You Tube), July 5, 2012, says, "You don't have to be rich to have a good time."

Cody Leonard says, "Games are good, but mind games are bad."

Kayden Carter says, "Be careful when you climb high it hurts when you fall."

Harbans says, "Just do what makes you happy."

SECOND EDITION ACKNOWLEDGEMENTS

Crazy Cousins was first printed November 2012 at Oscar's Books on Broadway and Granville in Vancouver. *Cape Lazo,* my previous novel had been such a success with friends, family, and colleagues that it seemed reasonable to print a couple hundred copies of *Crazy Cousins* (ISBN, bar code, "the works").

Oscar's Manager, Barry Bechta and I designed the front and back covers from photographs off my iPhone 3. The back cover was particularly pleasing because it was taken on a snowy day from Lacarno Beach. Gestalt-wise, if you looked closely you could see the silhouette profile of the "man on the beach." Not everyone could see it straight off, but with guidance it became clear.

The front cover showed Curlew Island at sunrise. We struggled with the book's body layout and after a couple iterations we arrived at a final version. We printed batches and distributed accordingly.

Sadly, Oscar's Books have gone out of business. Such fate has fallen upon many independent bookstores these days. My long-term advisor, R.S. Dinning, Attorney at Law, was terribly troubled with the thought of *Cape Lazo* and *Crazy Cousins* no longer in-print. Ron appears in *Cape Lazo* as a senior partner in the law firm Dinning, Maxwell and Meyers. Hence he has a bias. "Those books are like your children. You have to keep them alive."

Our friend Jeff Corigliano published *Terror Ridge* in 2012. Jeff liked my novels, but really disliked their layout and covers. "You *have* to go see my guy, Vladimir Verano at Third Place Press! Vlad can fix your book."

Three years later *Crazy Cousins* and *Cape Lazo* have gone to a second printing. Vladimir Verano at Third Place Press re-designed these two novels as well as my other novel *Belle Islet Lady*. All three are available in paperback and e-book format.

Many thanks to Vladimir and Third Place Press for your continued support and excellent service.

ABOUT THE AUTHOR

JOHN CARTER is a licensed psychologist, Adjunct Professor at UBC, and a slow paddler off the Mayne Island Coast. In addition to academic and psychological reports he writes novels: *Crazy Cousins*, *Belle Islet Lady*, and *Cape Lazo*.